You are richer today
if you have
laughed, given,
or forgiven.

–An Amish Proverb

MYSTERIES *of* LANCASTER COUNTY

AN UNBROKEN CIRCLE

MYSTERIES *of* LANCASTER COUNTY

Tricia Goyer *&* Cara Putman

Guideposts

New York

Mysteries of Lancaster County is a trademark of Guideposts.

Published by Guideposts Books & Inspirational Media
110 William Street
New York, NY 10038
Guideposts.org

Cover and interior design by Müllerhaus
Cover illustration by Bob Kayganich, represented by Deborah Wolfe, LTD.
Typeset by Aptara, Inc.

Printed and bound in the United States of America
10 9 8 7 6 5 4 3 2 1

AN UNBROKEN CIRCLE

CHAPTER ONE

The morning sun was nearing its zenith as Martha Classen Watts steered her car into the drive leading to her family home. A warm sense of satisfaction filled her when she saw at least a dozen cars and half as many buggies parked in front of the large barn that housed the combination thrift store and gift shop she and her two sisters had reopened ten or twelve weeks ago. Who would have guessed that, after Mama's funeral, she and her younger sister, Mary, would move back to Bird-in-Hand to live with their older sister, Elizabeth, in their childhood home and run Secondhand Blessings together? Martha liked to think the store was as popular now as it was when their grandparents started the business way back in the 1930s.

She gathered her handbag from the passenger seat and opened the door. A moment later, she stepped out of the car and then shifted to close the door. When she turned back to the red barn, Elizabeth was waiting for her.

"How was your trip into town?" she asked. "You had quite a few errands to run."

Martha nodded. "I got most everything done I needed to." And she had stayed busy. She didn't expect her sisters to remember, but two weeks from today would mark the second anniversary of Chuck's death. Becoming a widow at age fifty-three wasn't something she'd ever even contemplated, and some days it was harder to find joy than others.

She brought her thoughts back to the present. "Did we have many customers this morning?"

"Considering we've only been open an hour? Good enough."

Martha glanced at her watch. Was it really only eleven thirty? "You mean an hour and a half."

"I do." Elizabeth grinned and linked arms with Martha. The two walked to the store together, Elizabeth's khaki skirt brushing against Martha's leg.

The barn was built of wood planks painted a bright red. The building was open with a few items displayed on the wide door. Martha saw Mary sitting in one of the chairs in the small conversation nook the sisters had added to the shop. An Amish woman sat next to her, and the two were embroiled in a conversation.

Martha looked around the store's interior, and her heart sank as she realized little, if anything, from the detailed checklist she had written up had been accomplished. "You saw the list I pinned on the bulletin board in the office, right?"

Elizabeth nodded as she stepped away from Martha and shifted knickknacks around a table. "Of course. You only mentioned it five times at breakfast."

"And you got through the list?"

"I didn't say that. We've had a busy morning, as you can see."

Martha glanced around the interior. Handcrafted and antique furniture filled Elizabeth's favorite part of the store. Mary liked the children's area the best, with its bright colors and toys. The other sections included household goods, books, crafts, decorative items, tools, and jewelry, all displayed on beautiful Amish-made shelving. Clothing racks with gently used and vintage adult and children's clothing rounded out the eclectic atmosphere of Secondhand Blessings. Near the checkout counter and along one wall was Martha's display case, filled with scones, breads, cookies, muffins, and seasonal delights like jams, honey, and maple syrup. This addition to the thrift store inventory had been a hit. Once people tasted her marvelous cooking, they returned for more.

Martha tried to see the displays as customers walking in the door would, and what she saw made her fingers itch to get busy. Spring was fully behind them now, and June meant all things summer. Yet even though she'd left a to-do list that included updating their seasonal displays, there was Mary being Mary, sitting down and having what looked like a leisurely conversation with an elderly Amish woman. While she loved Mary, sometimes her younger sister's proclivity to sit and chat when there was work to be done could drive Martha crazy.

So much had to happen to make this endeavor a permanent part of their worlds. As Elizabeth left and came back in with the mail and a couple of packages, Martha sighed. At least her older sister was willing to be part of making Secondhand Blessings work. Martha moved to the table farthest from Mary and the Amish woman, who she could now see was Betty Yoder. Martha set to work straightening the table's contents. It might take a little creativity, but as she sifted through the accessories on the table, she began to see a summer theme emerge.

After the table was organized, Martha noted Betty had stood and was straightening her bonnet and smoothing her apron. Then she followed Mary to the counter where Elizabeth had just finished ringing up a customer. Betty held a quilt in her hands, and as Martha looked closer, she recognized it. The quilt was one that Anne Hostetler had shown interest in yesterday. Martha had all but promised Anne to hold it for her for a couple of days until Anne could figure out if she could afford it or not. In retrospect, maybe that hadn't been the best thing to do. Martha set down the teapot she'd been holding and hurried after Betty and Mary.

"I'm sorry, Betty, but I have an interested buyer in that quilt already." She turned to Mary. "Didn't you see the note I put beside it?"

"There wasn't a note, Martha." Mary stroked the quilt.

Elizabeth frowned. "Martha, you should have put it under the counter or in the back if it wasn't for sale."

"Yes, I can see that now. Well, that was my mistake, not Anne's, so I feel obligated to keep my word to her. She was so delighted to find it here."

One of Betty's eyebrows lifted, and she sniffed. "What did you promise this other customer? Mary here just promised it to me."

"I promised her I would hold it until tomorrow," Martha said. She touched Mary's arm. "You remember Anne Hostetler, Mama's friend, don't you? I can't go back on my word to her." She gently took the quilt from Betty and set it on the counter. "I'm sorry to disappoint you, but this one isn't available. I'll be glad to find you a similar one."

Betty's chin jutted. "Not good enough. This is the quilt I want." She folded her thin arms across her chest. "The quilt belongs to me, so you will have to call Anne Hostetler and tell her the quilt is sold. I do not want anyone else to have it, and especially not *her*."

Martha's eyes met Mary's, and questions filled her sister's gaze. Why was Betty acting this way, especially about Anne? Since Anne had been one of their mother's best friends, the three sisters had spent a lot of time with Anne, and she'd always been pleasant and kind. Obviously, Betty Yoder didn't view her that way. Martha was a bit taken aback by the Amish woman's open display of criticism.

"Betty, I can't do that." Martha fought the urge to mirror Betty's antagonistic posture. "I promised to hold it for her."

The defiance in the woman's eyes softened, replaced by a pleading look. "That quilt belonged to my family years ago. It was my *aenti* Melinda's. She never married and lived with my *dawdiss* until their deaths. As a child, I stayed at their home. I remember waking up and reading the scriptures on the quilt as the morning light beamed through the window." She smiled at the memory. "I loved running my fingers along the words, and before I knew it I'd memorized many of the verses. At some point the quilt disappeared, and I did not know what happened to it until now."

Elizabeth ran her hand over the quilt. "What makes you so sure this is that quilt, the one your aunt owned?"

"The verses are the same."

Martha took a closer look at the quilt. It was a crazy quilt, a random assortment of mismatched blocks that had various Bible verses embroidered on them. The blocks weren't the normal precise geometric blocks that were more common in the beautiful Amish quilts in the shops in Bird-in-Hand. Instead, it was a chaotic blend of different fabrics and styles of embroidery, each with a different Bible verse. The chaotic nature of the quilt actually added to its charm.

Mary appealed to Elizabeth. "Couldn't we at least talk to Anne about it? If the quilt was in Betty's family, maybe we should let her buy it."

Martha looked at Mary. "But Anne should still have first choice."

Mary's expression didn't waver. "Please."

Elizabeth looked from one sister to the other and then sighed. "All right. We can talk to Anne." She turned to Betty. "We can't make any promises about what she'll say."

"Thank you." Betty turned to leave. "Please let me know as soon as possible."

Martha sighed. "I'll get back to you as soon as I can, Betty." There was so much to do, but she would make time to call Anne. And when Anne said she still wanted the quilt, as Martha expected her to, this little tug-of-war would be over. The moment Betty exited the barn's door, Mary turned to Martha. "We have to get Anne to let us sell the quilt to Betty."

"Why?"

"Because it's a matter of heritage. If this quilt was Betty's aunt Melinda's, then we need to let her buy it. Maybe we should even let her have it."

"Mary." Martha shook her head. "We sell secondhand items. By definition, all those items belonged to someone already. If we start giving away items because they were once in someone's family, we'll never make a profit."

Elizabeth stepped between them. "How about I call Anne and see what she thinks. Surely if I explain everything to her, she'll decide to let Betty have the quilt." Elizabeth picked up the phone and dialed Anne's number. When Anne answered, Elizabeth moved to the corner to keep their conversation private. Martha knew Elizabeth would never do anything to embarrass Anne or make her feel as if the sisters were ganging up on her.

It was only a minute before Elizabeth put the phone down and walked back over to them, a frown marring her delicate features. "There's a problem, and I'm afraid Betty's mistaken. Anne says the quilt actually belonged to *her* family. She told me her cousin Irma made it. She also told me that she's not surprised that Betty would say otherwise."

How could two women have such a strong connection with the same quilt? Was one of them mistaken, or lying, about her connection to the piece? If so, which one, and why?

CHAPTER TWO

The hours flowed into the afternoon, but Martha's thoughts never strayed far from the quilt. How could Anne and Betty both have claims to the same one? It didn't make sense. The quilt was truly unique. It was impossible that two families could have the exact same quilt. It certainly wasn't one you would find in the pages of an Amish quilting book.

Could it be an Amish pattern that she hadn't seen before?

There was one person who might know.

Martha grabbed her purse. "I'd like to go talk to Rachel Fischer about the quilt. It shouldn't take long, and things seem to be pretty quiet. Would that be all right with you two?"

Elizabeth looked up from the box of new-to-them items she was sorting. "I think that would be all right, if you're not gone very long."

"We need to learn more about this quilt," Martha replied. "When we tell Betty that Anne still wants the quilt, we need to be able to tell her why."

"Don't be so certain, Martha." Elizabeth paused her sorting to meet Martha's gaze. "If the quilt came from Betty's family, that definitely affects who takes the quilt home."

"I don't know how we'll prove it one way or the other."

"Consider it a little mystery." Elizabeth shrugged. "I'm sure we'll be able to decipher who should have the quilt as part of her heritage. It shouldn't be that hard."

"I never would have thought before I moved here that we'd become Nancy Drews, but mysteries do seem to find us." Mary grinned at the sisters from her spot at the register.

"They do, don't they? And this one is very intriguing." As she walked out to her car, Martha wondered about Betty's motives. If it was so important to Betty and her family, then how had it come to be at Secondhand Blessings? If it was a treasure, surely the family would have taken steps to protect it. Or maybe it was only a treasure now that Anne wanted it. Martha had picked up on a dislike the two carried for each other.

She drove the short distance along the winding road to Rachel Fischer's house. The white clapboard home had a large garden to one side, a garden filled with the stunning colors of clematis, daylilies, and lithodora.

Rachel's twin eight-year-old boys were running around in the side yard, playing some sort of tag. Martha smiled at their exuberant play. It looked like they were delighted to be done with school for the day. She still couldn't quite comprehend how Rachel managed her home and her many children so well.

She parked and walked to the house. A cat lay curled up on the porch chair, and before she could knock at the door, it swung open and she found herself engulfed in a huge hug.

Phoebe, Rachel's twenty-year-old daughter, pulled back and smiled at Martha, her apron askew as if she'd started to take it off and then changed her mind. Her ever-joyful expression was all the welcome Martha needed, and she followed Phoebe into the house.

Rachel called from the kitchen. "Phoebe, bring our visitor into the kitchen, please."

When Phoebe turned to lead her to the kitchen, Martha noticed that Phoebe's apron was flour-dusted, and there was dough on the young woman's hands. She looked down at the front of her own shirt. Sure enough, there were patches of white on her navy blue blouse. She didn't even want to think of what was on her back. She chuckled. Phoebe's Down syndrome untethered her affections, which were offered freely and in abundance, even if they were a little messy at times.

When they walked into the kitchen, Rachel looked up from kneading bread dough on the table. Her eyes went wide, and her mouth dropped open. "Martha, please, do come in." She lifted her hands, which looked much like Phoebe's did. "Please excuse us—I was expecting Sarah Kauffman this afternoon, and I thought you were her." Rachel's chocolate-colored hair was brushed back under her white *kapp*, and her dress today was a deep purple color. The white work apron over the dress gave evidence that she'd been baking for quite a while. The aroma from the kitchen confirmed that. "But what a pleasant surprise. Please, sit down."

Martha smiled at her friend. "I'm so sorry for coming by unannounced. I didn't know how to let you know I needed to see you. Although I suppose I could have called and left a message on your phone out in the phone shack, but...well, I just couldn't wait. I need your help, your advice."

"Coming by as you did is perfect. Is all well?"

Martha looked around the large kitchen. The room truly was the heart of the home. Two of Rachel's children, thirteen-year-old Hannah and six-year-old Dorcas, sat at the table eating a snack. Martha assumed that the two older boys were working somewhere on the farm with their father. Something that smelled delicious was warming on the stove, and fresh chocolate chip cookies cooled on wire racks. Rachel gestured to two chairs placed in front of the fireplace. "Would you like coffee or tea as we chat?"

"If you have coffee made, that would be wonderful."

"I do." Rachel smiled at Phoebe. "Phoebe, would you please finish kneading this dough for me?" After washing her hands, Rachel went to the stove. She filled two mugs from the percolator on the back of the stove and brought one to Martha, just the way she liked it: black as the deepest night. "If it is too strong, let me know."

Martha inhaled the rich, slightly bitter aroma. "It's perfect."

Next Rachel slid several of the fresh cookies onto a plate and set it on the small table between the chairs before taking a seat. "How can I help you?"

Martha wasn't one who liked to ask for help, but sometimes it was necessary to push pride to the side. "We have a quilt in the store that two women are claiming as theirs. Anne Hostetler and Betty Yoder. Both women claim the quilt is a family heirloom, but that just can't be possible."

Rachel's eyebrows furrowed. "That *is* a challenge." She took one of the cookies before nudging the plate closer to Martha. "How can I help? I have been at many quilting circles—and I have visited most Amish homes in the area—but

I am far from knowing every quilt in the county, heirloom or new."

Martha grinned. "I wasn't expecting you to know who owned the quilt. I was simply hoping you might know a little more about the style."

Rachel's wrinkled brow smoothed. "Oh, that is better then." She winked. "*Ja,* well, I will see what I can do."

Martha pulled out her phone and tapped to pull up a photo of the quilt. Then she handed the phone to her friend. "Have you seen a quilt like this before? It's very unusual, but maybe it's more common than I thought."

Rachel took her time evaluating the photo. "It is unique."

"A crazy quilt?"

"Yes, most likely. Waste not, want not. It is not uncommon for someone to take the scraps leftover from a multitude of projects and create something that could look like this." She leaned closer and squinted. "Are those words?"

"Bible verses."

"Oh." Rachel leaned back. "I have seen something similar. I always thought of it as a sampler. A way that girls could practice and work on Bible memorization at the same time."

"Have you heard either Betty or Anne speak of such a quilt?"

"You must remember that Anne left the church when I was just a child. I have not had any occasion to go to her home." Rachel shrugged and handed Martha's phone back to her. "I do not remember seeing anything like this in Betty's home, but I cannot be certain I would have seen it anyway."

"Do you think one of the women is lying?"

Rachel's expression became stern. "Why would you think that?"

"They can't both be right." Martha hoped Rachel didn't think she was being critical. She just wanted to get to the bottom of the mystery and determine who should receive the quilt.

Rachel kept her lips pressed together, looked at the children sitting at the table, and lowered her voice. "I suppose this is not gossip and will help you understand the relationship between Anne and Betty. The two used to be close friends, confidantes even. Then Anne fell in love with Aaron, and they married and left the church." Rachel sighed. "Of course, Betty was obligated by the church to break off the friendship, but it does seem sometimes as if she took Anne's leaving as a personal offense against her."

Martha took a bite of her cookie, but her mind was on Rachel's words. "I remember Mama telling me about that. It sounds like it was a shock to the community. It's always hard when someone leaves the Amish, isn't it? I think those of us who aren't Amish don't understand the sense of betrayal very well. Mama explained those who leave are essentially leaving their family and community behind for good."

Rachel nodded. "I think it was even more shocking for Betty because they were such close friends, and she had no idea it was coming. Even though I know Anne had her reasons for leaving, I can understand Betty feeling as if she'd been betrayed."

Martha studied Rachel's face. She could tell it wasn't easy for her friend to talk about this. She patted Rachel's hand.

"That does help me understand both of them better. If only we could go through life without having to deal with such heartache." She sighed, thinking of her own loss.

"Ja, wouldn't that be nice? But I suppose our heartache causes us to lean into our Lord more. Ain't so?" She squeezed Martha's hand and then released it. "Now what other questions do you have about that quilt?"

"Betty mentioned that her aunt Melinda is the one who made this quilt. Did you ever meet her?"

"Of course. She and her family only lived over in Lancaster. Even for the Amish, ten miles is not an impossible distance. Melinda's youngest sister Hattie still lives there. Maybe you should talk with her."

Martha nodded. "I could take the quilt and ask if she remembers it."

Rachel studied Martha, and Martha forced herself to meet her friend's gaze. "Be careful not to jump to conclusions. It is best we hear what everyone has to say first. But you will be glad to know that Hattie lives in their family home. The one that Betty's aenti Melinda always called home."

As their visit concluded, Martha hoped that they would soon find the answers they were seeking. Yet inside she was torn. What if the quilt did belong to Betty? Would that change her mind? Martha wanted to honor her promise to Anne. It just seemed right. But how could she make that decision if someone's family heirloom was at stake?

CHAPTER THREE

A paw batting her nose knocked Elizabeth from a dreamless sleep. She generally loved all the animals that kept the home place so active and filled with personality, but as she set Butterscotch, Martha's loud orange tabby cat, to the side, she wished she could have slept a little bit longer. She needed the rest and the strength for what was sure to be a difficult day at the store.

She'd always felt in the middle of things when her sisters disagreed. How many hours of her childhood had she spent trying to help them see eye to eye and to find some common ground? Too many to count. Back then, Martha and Mary's squabbles were over chores and what television shows to watch. Now they were at odds over a quilt, and Elizabeth had no idea who was in the right. As Butterscotch flicked his tail to the side then looked back at her, Elizabeth sent up a silent prayer that some type of resolution concerning the quilt would happen soon. Then she turned her attention to the cat.

"Yes, your royal highness? Do you need something from me?"

He yowled and pranced to her bedroom door, which was open a crack. Apparently she didn't get it closed as tightly as she should have last night. That would teach her to make sure the latch caught. "Okay, okay, I'm getting up," she told the cat as he looked back at her with an impatient swish of his tail.

Elizabeth threw back the covers and slipped into the robe she'd left hooked over the bedside chair. With the coming of summer the temperatures climbed toward eighty during the day, but the nights were still chilly, especially in her room, where she had a cross breeze when she opened the windows. She padded from her room, down the hallway, and then down the stairs, through the kitchen and into the mudroom.

First things first. It was her job to feed the inside animals—two dogs and one very demanding cat. She refilled Butterscotch's food bowl and then his water bowl. Upon hearing the food pellets hit the bowl, Tinkerbelle, Mary's dachshund, and Pal, their border collie, raced to her, tails wagging. They had finally gotten Pal to quit stealing the other two's food, so they could all be fed together. Tinkerbelle paced back and forth in front of her bowl until Elizabeth poured in her food. As she filled Pal's dish, he brushed against her leg with his nose, as if thanking her.

Returning to the kitchen, Elizabeth filled the tea kettle with fresh water, set it on the stove to heat, and pulled out her Bible and journal. She looked at the chair across from her, thinking of the many mornings her mother had sat with her and they'd read the Bible together. She dearly missed such precious times. She turned to her mother's favorite passage, Psalm 23. She could almost hear Mama's voice. *"Elizabeth, sweetheart, never forget that the Lord is with you wherever you go."*

After she refilled her cup with hot water and a fresh tea bag, Elizabeth settled back at the kitchen table, and her thoughts quickly returned to their current mystery. Given the fact that both Anne and Betty claimed to remember seeing the quilt in their relatives' homes, Elizabeth figured that neither of them knew the whole story. While the quilt was beautiful, it hadn't been preserved as an heirloom. There was a raggedness to it. It had obviously been well-used, which supported Betty's recollection of it being on her aunt's bed.

She'd enjoyed reading the verses that had been embroidered on it, but the blocks didn't follow a discernible pattern. The stitches were uneven and scraggly. It was a slightly odd, discolored anomaly in a sea of beautiful Amish quilts. So many were like hand-sewn fine art. And this one wasn't. Any value the quilt held had to come from memories associated with it.

She glanced at the kitchen wall clock as she heard footsteps overhead. Her sisters must be beginning the day now. By the time she got up and brewed the coffee, Mary and Martha had joined her in the kitchen.

"Boy, do I need this." Martha took her mug in both hands and took a deep breath of the steam coming from it. "My dreams last night were all quilts, all the time. They were hanging everywhere—in the bathroom, in the kitchen, in the living room, in the office. They were beautiful, but...still."

Mary laughed. "That, my dear, is the sign of a guilty conscience. Your subconscious is trying to tell you something."

Martha rolled her eyes and grinned at her.

Elizabeth laughed with them. "We do have a mystery on our hands. And by now, we know the tried-and-true way to solve them. Talk to people. Dig for information." She rubbed her hands together. "So...who has time today to go talk to Betty and find out more about why she thinks this is her quilt?"

Mary sank into a chair at the table. "I wish I could, really I do. But Bill is coming by today to help me hang that batch of pictures we got last week. This is the only time he could make it this week, and I don't want to put it off any longer."

Elizabeth agreed with her. Bill Richmond was an old friend of the family, a local contractor, and a very nice guy. He and Mary had gone on a date recently, but as far as she knew, they were still on a just-friends basis.

She looked at Martha and raised her eyebrows.

Martha held her hands up. "Whoa, hold on there. I'm not the one who thinks Betty should get the quilt. Don't you think she might resent my coming to ask her a bunch of questions?"

Elizabeth thought about that. "I think you're just the right one to talk to her. Mary is already on her side, so she wouldn't ask the challenging questions that you would ask." She clapped her hands together. "That settles it. Mary, you and I will hold down the fort while Martha talks to Betty. I'll call her to make sure it's convenient to stop by this afternoon."

Martha put her coffee mug in the sink. "Well, I can't fault your logic. And I admit, there are a few questions I'd like to ask Betty. So yes, I'll go." She threw her hands up in the air. "Besides, what choice do I have? You've always been a bossy older sister."

Elizabeth grinned at her. "And don't you forget it," she said.

The sisters made and ate breakfast together, and then Elizabeth returned to her bedroom and got ready for the day. As soon as she could, she called Betty and left a message on the answering machine in Betty's phone shack. Not more than five minutes later Betty returned her call.

"I was out in the garden getting some strawberries for a pie when I heard the phone ring." Elizabeth could hear the smile in Betty's voice—so different than the anger of yesterday. "Did you say in the message one of you would like to stop over?"

"Martha would like to come, if it wouldn't be too much trouble."

"No trouble at all."

"Would one o'clock work for you?"

"I look forward to it."

With a smile on her face, Elizabeth went to find Martha and deliver the news. She had every expectation that this small mystery would be cleared up in no time and another Classen sisters dispute would be smoothed over. As the peacemaker in the family, she should know, right?

CHAPTER FOUR

After breakfast, Martha swept the porch and front walk. The morning air was humid, and the scent of rain was on the air. White clouds dotted the sky, causing a pattern of light and shadow on the ground. Martha's shoes crunched on the ground as she walked on the gravel path along the house. Even though only a few last flowers clung to the azalea bushes near the front of the house, she wanted to tend to them until the last bud fell.

Mary followed her out and waved as she headed to gather the eggs.

A minute later Mary emerged from the chicken coop with a smile and a full basket. "Ten eggs this morning."

"Sounds like the girls are happy."

Mary smiled. "I think so. Did Elizabeth find out whether or not you can go to Betty's this afternoon?"

"She did. I'll leave sometime after lunch. I can get my baking done this morning."

"I really appreciate your being willing to talk to Betty," Mary said. "Both of us just want to do the right thing. It's sad that one of those women is bound to be disappointed in the end."

Martha led the way into the house. "Hopefully we can find out the truth quickly, and both Anne and Betty will accept whatever that is."

The rest of the morning flew by. Martha eyed with satisfaction the loaves of poppy seed cakes and banana bread cooled and bagged on the counters alongside dozens of extra-large double-chocolate cookies.

Elizabeth rushed in for her lunch break. "I need to eat something in a hurry. Bill is due to come soon, and Della and the girls decided to come today with their haul instead of yesterday, so we have to get those sorted and recorded."

Martha went to the sink to wash her hands. "I'll make you a sandwich real quick. Are you sure I should leave this afternoon? Maybe it'd be better if I called Betty and postponed."

"No, let's keep to the plan." Elizabeth got the iced tea out of the fridge. "You know, I've been thinking that it might be a good idea to ask Rachel if she knows of a young Amish girl we could hire to help us in the shop. What do you think?"

Martha got the sandwich fixings from the fridge and opened the breadbox. "I think that's a great idea. Let's run it by Mary, and we can think on it and pray about it for a bit." She quickly assembled the sandwich, put it on a paper plate, and handed it to Elizabeth, who had just finished getting a glass of ice and pouring her tea. "There you go. Tell Mary I'll make her and Bill sandwiches and leave them on the counter."

Elizabeth took her glass in one hand and her plate in the other. She held the plate out to Martha. "And?"

Martha looked at her, puzzled. "And what?"

Elizabeth grinned. "I'm looking at a couple thousand of your famous double-chocolate cookies. Are you telling me you can't spare two for your favorite long-suffering, hardworking big sister?"

Martha laughed and scooped up three cookies. She put them on Elizabeth's plate. "Okay, since you're so pitiful." She snapped her fingers. "I think a few of these might sweeten up Betty too."

"If they don't, she can't be sweetened," Elizabeth said. "I better get out there." She whirled and rushed out of the kitchen. Martha made two more sandwiches, wrapped them in plastic wrap, and put them on a plate on the counter along with half a dozen cookies. She plated another half a dozen for Betty and covered them also. She then grabbed her purse from its spot and hurried outside to her car. It didn't take long to reach Betty's small house.

As she parked and walked to the front door, Martha noted that the house was well kept and that an abundant garden of annuals ran along the front of the house. A river of soft pink, white, and orange flowers ran into one another without end. The front door opened followed by the screen banging.

Betty stepped onto the small front porch. "Glad you could find me."

Martha smiled as she stepped forward. "I'm getting better at finding places, although things have certainly changed in the decades I've been away." She stepped inside as Betty held the door. The inside was clean and spare. A quilt hung on the back of the sofa—the only splash of personality and color in the room. "Thank you for seeing me."

"Did you bring the quilt?"

There was so much hope in that sentence that Martha hated to tell her no. "I'm here to learn more so we can settle where the quilt goes."

"Why? It has to come here. It was made by my aenti."

"But how do you know that for certain? Anne is convinced it's exactly like the one that was in her family. She says her cousin made it."

"That is easy. Anne is wrong." Betty paced toward the kitchen. "Would you like coffee?"

"That would be nice." Martha stood where she was in the living room as Betty went to work in her small kitchen. Martha eyed the oil lamps that hung from the ceiling. Even though it was dim inside the house, they weren't lit. Instead, the natural light from the window warmed the room. "Can I do anything to help?" she called to Betty.

"Just have a seat. This will not take a minute." After a short wait, Betty brought a tray of coffee with sugar and cream to the small table by the couch. "Have a seat, please," Betty repeated.

Martha settled on the small chair near the sofa and then accepted the mug from Betty. "So, what can you tell me about the quilt?"

"My aenti Melinda made it."

"How do you know it was this quilt?"

Betty leaned back and took a sip of her coffee. "There were verses on her quilt. I remember Aenti Melinda teaching me to read by helping me sound out the letters in the verses."

"Wow."

"And as I said before, I slept under it many a night. My aenti was an incredible woman. She never married or had kids of her own, so she had tons of love to pour into her nieces and nephews."

Martha thought of her own three kids and how they adored Elizabeth, who had doted on them all their lives. "Do you remember which verses were on it?" If Betty's memory matched the quilt, that could be evidence the quilt was the one she remembered.

"Verses like Proverbs 3:5. 'Trust in the Lord with all thine heart,' and First Peter 5:7, 'Casting all your care upon him; for he careth for you.' That one was the whole verse, but most of them were snippets of verses because they had to fit on a quilt square. Oh, and I remember one about mounting up with wings as eagles. Another about not letting your heart be troubled. I think that was from one of the gospels."

"Any that were unusual?"

"I remember there was one from Habakkuk." She smiled. "I just remember how funny that word was to sound out. It made me giggle every time."

Martha smiled back at her. "It sounds like a wonderful memory."

Betty sighed. "I know it is not much, but it has been years since I have seen that quilt."

"When was the last time you saw it—before seeing it in the shop, that is?"

"Oh, I cannot say. I remember that quilt being on Aenti Melinda's bed for years." Betty played with the handle of her mug. "But it has been almost thirty-something years since she died."

"Then how did it move from her home?"

"I will admit that is a mystery to me. As I said, I remember it being on her bed for years. Then one time when I came, it was not." Betty shrugged. "When I asked her about it, she said that she'd spilled juice on it, and her sisters had gotten her a new quilt for Christmas to replace it. I guess I never really thought about what she did with it."

"Did you see it again after that?" Martha tried to capture everything Betty was saying so she could share it later with her sisters. So far, Betty hadn't said anything that made it conclusive that the quilt was her aunt Melinda's.

"I cannot say that I did. I guess I assumed she had put it in a closet somewhere."

"Did she have her initials or name somewhere on the quilt? Something like that would really help us know that this is her quilt."

"There is nothing like that as far as I remember, though it would not surprise me to know I forgot a detail like that."

"I can check the quilt carefully when I get back." In fact, she would do that right away. That could be a very easy solution to the mystery.

Martha collected her purse and stood. "Thanks again for letting me come over." It felt like all she was leaving with was a list of Bible verses to check against the quilt. Although that alone wasn't a definitive answer either.

But as she walked to her car another scripture verse filled her mind. *If any of you lacks wisdom, you should ask God.* She had a feeling that was the verse they should be relying on.

CHAPTER FIVE

Martha got back to the shop in time to fill her display cases for the afternoon rush. Right before closing, she'd sold out of the cookies and most of the bread. She stepped outside and let the early summer breeze cool her face. It was nice to see her baked goods selling well, yet she was still trying to find the rhythm of how much of which items to bake on which days. She'd been playing with having certain items on dedicated days, and so far it seemed that was working well. It kept her from going quite as crazy trying to bake a little bit of multiple varieties each day or two.

She tucked a strand of hair behind her ear and lifted her face to the sky. It was a rich blue, providing a vibrant backdrop for the rich, early summer foliage. Summer had arrived, and she loved the green that coated the trees and stretched to the horizon.

Elizabeth came out of the shop and waved to Martha to come back. "How did your meeting go?"

Martha sighed. "Not as well as I'd hoped. I'm not sure how we'll determine whose quilt this is." She took Elizabeth's arm and pulled her back inside the barn. "But we can't give up yet. I still have a few ideas to check out before I give up." She let go of Elizabeth's arm, and Elizabeth followed her as she wove among the tables and past Mary, who was helping a couple of women at the kitchenware table.

As she passed the tables, Martha noticed that several were getting low on goods. Time to let the consigners know they could bring in more items, and time to work on getting the goods they purchased from estate auctions and other sales on display. Elizabeth echoed her thoughts. "We need to get the estate sale items out here. You know, the ones Angelina gave us last week."

Martha stopped suddenly. "Angelina! That's who we should ask about the quilt. Wasn't it in that batch of items from that sale? Now where did we put the quilt?"

Elizabeth pointed to the counter Billy had made for them. "It's on the shelf beneath the counter. And you're right. We need to find out from Angelina whose estate sale it was."

Martha retrieved the quilt and carried it to a long table in the back. "Well, right now I want to see if we can find any marks that identify the maker."

"Like initials?"

"Exactly. Or maybe the maker embroidered her name on the front border or the back." Martha started to pull the quilt open across the table. "Betty also told me the verses she remembers that were on her aunt's quilt. If we can find those verses on this quilt, then it could be the one she remembers."

"Unless they're popular verses."

"Possible. But she told me quite a few of them. I believe it would be too much of a coincidence to have all of them on more than one quilt, wouldn't it?"

Elizabeth helped her spread out the quilt. "What verses are we looking for? That would be the easier place to start."

"Betty mentioned the one about mounting up with wings as eagles."

"Isn't that somewhere in Isaiah?"

"I think so."

"That's a good one. It's a favorite of Mary's." She pointed to a blue patterned square. "There it is. Isaiah 40:31."

"She said Proverbs 3:5 was on it."

"That one's over here." Elizabeth pointed to a pink sprigged calico that had a muslin embroidered square over it with the words about trusting in God.

"Yes, that's it." Martha lifted her gaze, trying to remember the other verses. "Also First Peter 5:7." She turned back to the quilt and ran her hand over several patches. "Ah, here's that one. Do you see the one about 'let not your heart be troubled'?"

Elizabeth pointed to one of the corners. "Yes, that one is here. John 14:27. The verses she mentioned are on here. But there are a lot more. Do you think the quilt she remembers was this big?"

"She said it was on her aunt's bed for years, so I guess that's about this size." She eyed the quilt. The blocks were all different styles, and the embroidery didn't look the same. "It's as if this quilt was made by different people."

"Or the same person with different levels of expertise." Elizabeth bent closer. "Now let's look at each square and the border carefully to see if we can find any maker's marks."

Martha carefully examined her half of the quilt. There wasn't anything in any of the squares that looked like initials or a person's name. The border was equally void of hints. "Maybe there's something on the back."

"Maybe." But Elizabeth sounded as hopeless as Martha felt. The sisters worked together to lift the quilt and flip it to the back. The plain muslin had what looked to be a water stain over a portion of the left side. Martha remembered that Betty said her aunt's quilt had gotten juice spilled on it, but since the Amish made quilts to be used, she figured most of them at one time or another got soiled by something spilling on them. Other than the one stain, there wasn't anything on the back of this one. Elizabeth dropped the edge she was examining. "Well, that wasn't too helpful."

Martha wasn't ready to give up. This particular little mystery was keeping her mind off the events of two years ago that had forever changed her life. "We'll just have to keep trying. It seems as if this quilt has a story for us—one we can't understand yet." Martha ran a hand along the back. The fabric was soft, as if it had been washed many times. The comfortable feeling that came from a well-used and well-loved item. "We'll figure this out, Elizabeth. If the quilt belongs to one of these families, we'll find out and get it to the right family. If not, then it will make a lovely addition to Anne's home."

"And Betty will be disappointed."

"About a quilt. In the big scheme of things, this isn't anything that will change a person's life." Martha smiled to soften her words. "But what does it hurt for us to do what we can to learn the history of the quilt?"

The sisters worked into the early evening hours trying to get caught up by cataloging some of the items a consigner had brought in the prior week. Martha was tasked with sorting the items so that Mary could record them in the ledger book and Elizabeth could assign them space in the shop. The sorting work gave her hands something to do while her mind tried to determine how they could learn more about the quilt. They had learned that it wasn't unusual for an Amish woman to make a scripture quilt. But certainly the "crazy" patterns and materials made this particular quilt unique.

One thing was clear. The quilts that had been in Anne's and Betty's families were memorable to them as much more than a simple bed covering. She thought about the somewhat awkward stitches on some of the squares and the verses that were embroidered on them. Each square held such rich meaning. The scriptures were reminders to anyone who saw them day in and day out, sealing those promises into one's heart over time.

That would certainly add to the sentimental value of the quilt.

Mary got up from where she was sitting cross-legged on the floor and started to walk to the back of the barn, where they kept their inventory. Martha stopped her. "Do you remember if Angelina said which estate sale this quilt came from?"

Mary paused and considered the question. "No, I don't remember her mentioning whose it was. Would you like me to check the records?"

"Yes. Maybe that will help us figure out where the quilt originated."

Mary nodded and continued on her errand. A few minutes later, she wandered back to where Martha was finishing up for the night. "I didn't find anything. Are you thinking that we should ask Angelina where it came from?"

"Yes. And didn't she say something about only giving us the items she thought we would want?"

"I think so. She made it sound like she had quite a bit more somewhere else, but that she thought we would be most interested in what she brought us. What are you thinking?"

"I'm thinking that maybe there's an item we didn't see that could give us some clues." Martha tapped her chin with her finger as she considered what else might be useful to learn from Angelina.

Angelina Raymond was an estate liquidator they had started working with over the last month or so. So far, it had been a relationship that worked well for both sides. The arrangement provided Angelina with a rather ready market for some of the items she discovered, and the sisters had received some nice collections to sell.

"I'll look up the number and give Angelina a call." Martha boxed up her supplies and organized the counter space so it would be ready when they came in the next morning. She rolled her head slowly and raised her shoulders.

Mary watched her and winced. "Got a crick in your neck?"

"Yeah." Martha grinned. "Just wait till you reach my age, little sis. You only have a few more years of being able to do your work on the floor. Getting up is a lot harder than getting down, let me tell you."

Mary laughed. "I'll take your word for it until the day you have to pull me up." Then she sobered. "I wanted to tell you again how much I appreciate your talking to Betty today. I know how important it is to you that Anne doesn't think you're going back on a promise."

Martha waited for Elizabeth to join them, and they walked toward the shop door. "I'll just be glad to figure out who to sell the quilt to. Maybe we'll know more after I reach Angelina. I wonder who else we should talk to."

Mary reached for the lights to flip them off. "I don't know. Maybe after we talk to Angelina, we'll get ideas."

Elizabeth exited the barn and waited for the other two to join her before pulling the door closed and locking it. "I hope so, but Betty didn't point Martha toward anyone else."

Mary took her sisters' arms. "Half the fun of a mystery is figuring out who has the clues. We'll talk to more people. This mystery doesn't stand a chance. Not with the Classen sisters on the job. The game's afoot, girls."

As they entered the house, Martha heard the truth in Mary's words. If they asked the right questions they'd uncover the quilt's provenance. And then, they'd know who to sell it to...she hoped.

CHAPTER SIX

The next morning Martha was partway through cleaning up her baking mess when her cell phone buzzed with a text from Mary. CUSTOMER HAS AN IDEA ABOUT SOMEONE WE SHOULD TALK TO ABOUT THE QUILT. A moment later, that message was followed by a second. SAYS THE WOMAN'S NAME IS HATTIE SCHRAEDER. SHE'S LIVED IN THE AREA FOREVER. KNOWS EVERYONE. After that, a third text contained an address in Lancaster.

Martha texted back DO YOU HAVE A NUMBER?

Her phone buzzed again. NO, SHE'S AMISH. CUSTOMER SAYS MAYBE PHONE IN SHACK, BUT DOESN'T HAVE NUMBER FOR IT.

Could this Hattie be the same one that was a sister to Betty's aunt Melinda? If so, it was definitely worth connecting with her and learning what she knew.

Twenty minutes later, after checking with her sisters to make sure they had the shop covered, Martha placed the quilt on the passenger seat and set out for the address Mary had sent her. The drive was pleasant, with her GPS only getting her turned around once.

Would the Lancaster area ever feel like home again? Would she retire the maps and apps and find where she was going because she knew the community and belonged? She hoped that day came quickly. She didn't enjoy feeling like she was still a visitor in her own hometown.

When she pulled into the driveway of a small house, she double-checked the address. An older-model navy sedan sat in front of the house, and the barn looked abandoned. GPS said this was the correct place, but it didn't feel Amish. Maybe the GPS had gotten confused. This wouldn't be the first time.

Martha pulled the quilt from the car and approached the front door. Large butterfly bushes loaded with vibrant purple blossoms edged the small front porch on either side. They provided a nice contrast with the plain white paint on the house.

She stepped up to the door and knocked. After a few moments, she knocked again.

"Coming." A reedy voice reached her through the closed door. After another moment, the door eased open with a squeak of the hinges. A small woman, white hair covered by a prayer kapp, smiled at her with a question in her eyes. "Can I help you?"

"You can if you are Hattie Schraeder. My name is Martha Classen Watts.'My sisters and I have a shop in Bird-in-Hand, and I have a few questions about a quilt."

"I am Hattie Schraeder, so you are in the right place. A quilt? I am not sure how I can assist, but please come in, and I will see what I can do." She stepped back.

Martha followed her into the tidy space. Hattie looked to be in her eighties, but she walked with the light step of some-one twenty years younger. A crocheted afghan in oranges and yellows adorned the back of a small couch. Gingham curtains hung from the windows in the living room and kitchen, spaces separated by a small half wall. A wooden rocker sat in front of a small fireplace that had a few logs waiting for a light. Martha waited until Hattie eased onto the rocker.

"All right, Mrs. Watts. What can I do for you?" Hattie adjusted her glasses and peered at Martha.

"Please, call me Martha. A quilt came into our shop a few weeks ago. I put it on display, and Anne Hostetler came in and expressed interest in buying it. Then Betty Yoder came in and wanted it as well." Martha sat down on the edge of the couch and laid the quilt beside her. "They both tell us that the quilt came from their family."

"Interesting." Hattie watched her. "Is that what you brought with you?"

"Yes. Can I show you the quilt?" She patted the fabric, then shifted it to her lap. "This quilt is unique, so I don't know how both women can be certain it was made by someone in their families."

"Let me see that."

Martha stood and stretched the quilt across the top of the afghan and over the couch. She adjusted the edges then stepped back to give Hattie a hand. The petite woman waved her away.

"Why do you think I took the rocking chair?" She grinned as she leveraged the chair forward and stood. "Let me see this quilt." She stepped forward and fingered the fabric. "Definitely calico, maybe even flour sack fabric."

"That might be right. If the quilt was made in the early 1900s." Martha shrugged. "We don't know enough yet to know if it was crafted then."

Hattie leaned closer and examined the stitches. "Well, this looks almost like a starter quilt. The kind a girl would work on when she was learning to quilt, learning embroidery." She ran her fingers along the edge where two blocks came together. "I would about call this a crazy quilt."

"It certainly doesn't have a pattern I could find in a book."

"Not all quilts do. Sometimes one creates what is in her heart." Hattie smiled. "I remember learning to quilt. It was a chore and a privilege. All those hours sitting trapped by fabric. Yet I knew at the end of it, I'd see something that would warm my bed. My stitches probably were not this tight on my first one. How I loved that quilt."

"I quilted a log cabin pillow." That was about all the patience Martha had for the task. She was constantly amazed by the amount of work that went into each completed quilt. A true labor of love.

"That is a start." Hattie smiled at her, then turned back to the quilt. "My sister Melinda made a quilt like this. It was quite a crazy quilt." Hattie studied the quilt for a moment. "I do remember it looking something like this one—I have a vague memory—although it has been so many years. I imagine I have helped sew hundreds of quilts at sewing circles since then."

"Melinda Yoder was your sister?"

"My much older sister." Hattie smiled as she returned to her rocking chair. "She liked to quilt, but always said that a crazy quilt was her starter. I liked it but never made one myself."

"And does that mean Betty Yoder is your niece?"

"Yes, I have a niece named Betty. I was not sure that was the Betty Yoder you were talking about when you mentioned the name. I know four Betty Yoders, and all of them live within a few miles."

"Do you have any photos of the quilt?" Martha was so excited to know the answer that she didn't realize her misstep until after the words had escaped. "I'm sorry. I keep forgetting..."

Hattie waved her apology aside. "It is no worry. It has been so long since I have seen it, I do not know that I could describe it well. There are no photographs either."

"Of course." She knew the Amish didn't take photos, she really did. Even if she had forgotten in the moment. One good photo could have ended the question about whether the quilt was a match to the one Betty remembered. What now? "How did Melinda get the idea for the quilt?"

"I really do not know. You have to understand, Melinda was the oldest daughter, and I was the youngest. There was a twenty-five year span between us." Hattie leaned back in the chair, and it gently started moving. "I am not sure if she was the sister who told me, or if it was another one, but I heard some time ago about a circle of friends who sent quilt blocks to each other and then shared the finished quilt through the years. Maybe something like that would explain the varied styles and stitches. If it happened once, it likely happened in multiple groups."

"What do you mean by a circle?"

"A group of friends connected by something they have in common. Maybe they were born the same month or had the same name. Sometimes girl cousins around the same age would join a circle together. The reasons they started are as many as you can think of. I was in one as a young girl. We were all the last born of many brothers and sisters."

"That's quite a connection."

"It made sharing pieces of our lives fun. We could relate to the chaos of large families and the fear of being lost at the end." She tugged her glasses down and wiped her eyes. "But we simply shared letters. I know other groups shared little things. Things that could be easily mailed."

Martha turned to the quilt and noted the size of the blocks. "It would be possible to mail the quilt blocks."

"Yes. How many verse blocks are there?"

"Fifteen. Three across and five lengthwise, with enough border and space in between the blocks to make a nice-size bedspread."

"Depending on how many girls in the circle, they each could easily have mailed three or four squares to the girl charged with assembling the quilt."

"How do I find out about that?"

"I do not know that you can." Hattie met her gaze. "You can ask Betty if she remembers Melinda ever talking about a circle that exchanged quilt squares. And talk to Anne too. You said Anne Hostetler, right? The woman who left the church?"

"Yes, that is the Anne Hostetler. I'm amazed at your memory."

Hattie tapped the side of her head. "I do remember she and Aaron were part of the church and then they were not. It does not happen too often, you see—or at least it did not happen as much years ago—but when it does happen, everyone is shocked." The woman sighed as if seeing something from the past. "But yes, ask Anne too. She might know if there was a circle that—whoever Anne believes made the quilt—was a part of. If so, it might be your answer."

Martha gathered the quilt and stood. "Thank you for your time."

Hattie pushed to her feet. "My pleasure. I always welcome company."

"Does anyone live with you?"

Hattie chuckled. "I have family a quarter mile down the road. That is close enough for now. I like my independence." She walked to the door, and Martha followed. "Please come back if you have more questions." She flexed her fingers. "I have quilted many a quilt with these fingers."

"I will do that. I appreciate your help." A minute later, as she pulled out of the drive and started back to Secondhand Blessings, Martha waved at the small woman. She would like to learn more about these circles. She still wasn't sure if she completely understood. It sounded like more than pen pals, but maybe not. Someone would be able to explain the concept more fully. Maybe Rachel could explain it better the next time Martha saw her.

As soon as she reached the barn, Martha tucked the quilt back in its protective bag and settled it on a table in the office space. Then she sat at the desk and pulled over the stack of files with current invoices, poring over them in search of a familiar name. She found the number for Angelina and placed the call. After a couple of rings, a woman answered. "Raymond Estate Services."

Martha wished she knew the woman well enough to know her voice. "Is this Angelina?"

"Yes."

Martha quickly explained what she needed.

"I still have many of the estate items here. You're welcome to come look through them."

"That would be great, thank you. Would tomorrow after five work?"

"Sure. I'm usually here until at least six thirty most nights."

Martha confirmed the address. "Thank you, we'll see you then." And maybe they'd find something definitive about the quilt's ownership and history.

How did a quilt that was so desperately wanted by two parties end up in the estate sale of a third? It was a mystery indeed.

CHAPTER SEVEN

The doors to Secondhand Blessings stood open, welcoming a warm breeze as the sisters greeted customers and went about the dozens of small tasks that came with running a busy thrift shop. Martha knew that, soon enough, they would have to think about turning on the air conditioning. It was going to get too hot to leave the doors open all summer, although that is what her grandparents and parents had done in years past. Their Amish customers didn't seem to mind the heat, but if they wanted to keep their Englisch clientele happy, they needed to think about creature comforts.

She set to work, organizing items of clothing that had been picked through more than once that morning. Suddenly her hands stilled, and then slowly lowered to the table, clutching the man's shirt she'd been folding. Her heart was racing, and she was back in Kansas, back in her laundry room, folding one of Chuck's shirts. She'd just picked up the basket to carry it into the bedroom when she heard the phone ring. She'd answered it and heard news that shattered her heart and then her world.

"Excuse me?"

Martha blinked and set her shoulders before she turned and saw a young Amish woman with a small child on either side of her and a baby in her arms. "Can you help me find board books with farm animals in them?"

"Of course." Martha led the young woman to the bookshelves, where she helped her sort through the children's section. They found three board books that the children latched on to, and Martha offered the grateful young mother a deal for all three. After checking her out at the register, she looked up and saw Rachel coming in the door, clutching a basket.

"The wind is picking up out there. It looks as if we are in for a storm." Several leaves followed Rachel through the door, as if to make her point. She held out the basket toward Martha once she was inside. "Here are the doilies that I repaired for you. Most of them are back to like new. A few have more character."

Martha accepted the basket and flipped through a handful of the lace. "You did a beautiful job with these. Thank you."

"It is my pleasure. Do you need anything else repaired or cleaned?"

"Not that I know of, but I'll ask Elizabeth after I get you a check." She led Rachel to the counter and set the basket in front of Mary. "Look at what Rachel accomplished."

Mary oohed and aahed over the delicate pieces. "These really came back to life. It will be easy to sell them now."

Martha pulled the checkbook from its spot in the cash register. "How much did we agree to?"

Rachel told her the amount, and after writing the check and giving it to her, Martha went to find Elizabeth. She finally located her in the back of the shop, dusting and straightening the paintings and needlework samplers. "Elizabeth, Rachel is here. Do we have anything else we need her to work on for us?"

Elizabeth straightened and arched her back before slowly twisting from side to side. "I don't think I have anything for her now, but I do have a question for her. I'll come with you." She wiped her hands on one of the cheesecloth rags she kept in a pile. "First, though...how do the doilies look?"

"Beautiful. We can give her more work and know she'll do a great job."

"Good. It will be nice to let her handle more of the textiles from now on so we can work on other items." Elizabeth smiled when she reached the front counter. "Rachel! Martha was just telling me what a great job you did."

"It was nothing. Sometimes using the older ways are a benefit when working with older items." She nudged the basket toward Elizabeth. "I would like to know that all of you are satisfied with my work."

Elizabeth looked through the doilies, taking the time to inspect the work and point out where Rachel had removed a stain or fixed a snag. As Martha watched Rachel beam, she wished she'd thought to do that. Mama had always said not to underestimate the power of praise for a job well done.

Elizabeth removed the last doily and then edged the basket back to Rachel. "We would be delighted to work with you on other items as they come in." Then she leaned on the counter as Mary slipped from behind it to wait on a customer at the bakery display case. "Would you have time for a cup of coffee? We need to ask you a couple of questions."

"Sure." Rachel looked between Elizabeth and Martha. "Is anything wrong? Is one of you sick?"

"Nothing like that," Martha assured her. "I visited Hattie Yoder this morning."

"Oh." Rachel watched Martha with a quizzical expression.

"She remembered her sister Melinda having a quilt like the one we have, but she didn't have photos or anything."

"Of course not."

Martha prepared three mugs of coffee. She handed one to Elizabeth, one to Rachel, and kept one for herself. "Anyway, she mentioned something that I hoped you could help us understand. What is a circle?"

Rachel's brows furrowed, and she looked confused. "You mean the shape?"

Elizabeth looked confused too.

"No, Hattie made it sound like a group that had something in common and might send things to each other."

Rachel's puzzled look cleared. "Oh, you mean like letters? I have heard of circle letters. Amish girls used to exchange those many years ago."

"That sounds really interesting—and fun." Elizabeth took a sip of her coffee. She turned to Martha and caught her eye. "Thanks for this, Martha."

"You're welcome." After Martha set her own mug down, she returned her attention to Rachel. "I'm not sure exactly what it is, but Hattie thought this particular circle might have exchanged quilt squares."

Rachel frowned. "I suppose it is possible, but I have never heard of such a circle. The one I was in as a young girl simply exchanged letters."

A gust of wet wind blew through the open barn door, along with three women with their purses held over their heads. Elizabeth jumped to her feet and waved to the three women, who entered the store, and then she hurried their direction to close the door. "Welcome to Secondhand Blessings. Can we help you?"

While Elizabeth tended to the customers, Martha continued her conversation with Rachel.

"It looks like the quilt might belong to Betty after all. She was able to tell me some of the scriptures that were embroidered on the quilt. I wonder if I should ask Anne if she can remember the scriptures. If she can't, maybe she's wrong about the quilt."

Rachel shifted and shook her head. "I do not agree. Just because Anne might have a bad memory or might not have seen it often in her youth doesn't mean the quilt isn't hers. And you do not need to be in a hurry to decide. Neither Betty nor Anne should mind a delay if it means you locate the history of the quilt. Then the decision of who owns it will be simple."

Before Martha could answer, Elizabeth and Mary joined them. "I sold the rest of your muffins, Martha," Mary said. "That woman asked for three, but when I gave her the bag, she opened it, took a whiff, and decided to buy the rest." She smiled with warmth as she looked between the women. "I think I could have sold her twice as many if I'd had them."

Rachel retrieved her basket and nodded to Elizabeth. "Thank you for the work. If you need help in the future, let me know." She smiled. "And Martha, think about what I said. I have a feeling this mystery will not be solved overnight."

Mary tilted her head to the side. "What did you say?"

"Just that you don't have enough evidence to make any conclusions about who owns the quilt yet. And that there's no hurry to decide." Rachel twisted one of her kapp strings around her finger. "This might take weeks to figure out."

Mary gasped, and her eyes widened. "Weeks? You have to be joking, right?" She shook her head and turned to Martha. "No, we can't wait that long. We need to find some answers. Betty is really hurting over this."

Elizabeth's jaw dropped, as if she was surprised by Mary's outburst. Redness rushed to Mary's cheeks as if she had surprised herself. Martha couldn't help but smile. "Mary, when did you decide that we needed to pass along the quilt in such a hurry?"

Mary sighed. "I'm just eager for us to find the rightful owners and move on."

Even though everyone seemed to find the humor in Mary's outburst, it was clear the dueling claims bothered her. Was that even a hint of tears in her eyes?

Martha's heart softened to her sister. Even as a young girl, conflict had bothered Mary. And Martha knew that Mary's desire to smooth away conflict was stronger because she couldn't fix her marriage with Brian. She could see that Mary wanted a solution that was quick and smooth so no one would be hurt and where the relationship between them wouldn't be strained. Martha wanted her younger sister to understand that even though there were varying opinions about what to do with the quilt, it was a minor conflict. This wasn't going to put a large rift between them, even if they disagreed at times.

Elizabeth's heart must have softened too, because Martha saw a new tenderness in Elizabeth's gaze. Elizabeth reached over and patted Mary's hand. "We all want to do what's right, for both Anne and Betty."

"Yes, I know we do," Mary admitted. "But it's just a blanket, right?"

As soon as Mary said the words, Martha knew her baby sister had a lecture coming her way.

Rachel shook her head. "A quilt is not simply a piece of fabric that covers your bed. It is a treasure that is handed down in families from generation to generation. It is a tie to the past and to family history. It is much more than just a blanket."

Elizabeth patted Mary's arm. "See? This is why Rachel is right. The quilt is part of some family's history, and we need to take our time to find the right family."

While that sounded noble, Martha didn't know how they'd find the answer. And as she watched her sister, she knew Elizabeth didn't either.

CHAPTER EIGHT

Elizabeth held on to her skirt as she walked toward the mailbox in the wind that foretold another coming storm. She waved at the mail carrier as he pulled away from the box. A few steps and she was at the box. She pulled the mail out and sorted through it as she walked back to the shop.

There was so much junk mail that she almost missed the small envelope mixed among the stack. She didn't recognize the handwriting, and there was no return address, so she flipped it over, looking for anything on the back. It was blank. But since it was addressed to the store rather than one of her sisters, she slid a finger beneath the flap as she shouldered her way into Secondhand Blessings.

Mary looked up from her spot by the kitchenware table. "Sounds like it's getting serious out there."

"This storm is letting us know it's almost here." Elizabeth waved the mail at Mary. "I'm going to put what isn't junk in the office."

"All right."

As she walked to the office, Elizabeth tugged the small card from the envelope. It was blank except for a short message in beautiful, almost calligraphic penmanship. She tossed the junk in the recycle bin and then settled on a chair as she read the short note.

Thank you for your help selling my mother's estate items. It was so nice to have that handled and so well. Arlene Smyth

Elizabeth read the words again. The items from that estate hadn't been numerous or terribly involved. Martha had found a good price for each with a minimal amount of research, working her miracles with the internet. They'd then posted the estate items on a few lists and had sold almost every item within a matter of weeks. The check had been nice for the family.

She wanted to do that with the crazy quilt—find a similar wonderful outcome. Until they went to visit the estate liquidator later that afternoon, they were at a standstill on learning more about the quilt. They'd already examined it, and Elizabeth didn't think they'd missed anything significant. It was a quilt—a little odd, but still charming with its Bible verses. She set the card on the desk for Mary and Martha to read later and glanced at Martha's to-do list before returning to the shop.

The morning hours passed slowly then, after lunch, Martha hurried in with her box of muffins, homemade granola bars, and scones. Each was packaged in a cellophane bag with a thin ribbon on top of the twist tie. Martha put the items in the display case and then dusted her hands off on her jeans. "Where do you need me today?"

Mary looked between her sisters. "I think we've got it right now."

"She's right. I even knocked one item off your list." Elizabeth smiled as she nodded toward the office. "You might like a card we got this morning. From the Smyth estate. It's in the office."

Martha smiled back at her. "Yes, well, wonderful. It seems as if we're really getting the hang of things, aren't we?" She looked at her watch. "Do you mind if I tackle a project I've been itching to get at for a while?"

Hope buoyed in Elizabeth's heart seeing the excitement on her sister's face. She clasped her hands together. "Oh, please tell me it's that old dresser you started sanding down—the one from the same estate as the quilt? It could become a delightful dresser for a child's nursery."

Martha ran a hand through her hair, her eyes twinkling. "Yes, I was thinking it would too. I'm eager to get it fixed up. I think all those makeover shows inspire me. I even bought some chalk paint in the prettiest robin's-egg blue."

Mary approached, a wistfulness in her eyes. "Oh, could you imagine how excited a new mom would be to discover such a find?" She raised one hand straight up into the air. "My vote is that you work on the dresser today. At least until it's time to go see Angelina."

Elizabeth moved in the direction of the back room. "I can work at getting those drawers out for you—to make it easier to paint. I know that lower one was sticking..."

"Yes. I'd like that. Thank you." Martha moved to the back office area to gather her supplies. "I'll be there in a moment to help you."

Elizabeth reached the back room and moved to the dresser. It appeared to be handmade and had to be at least sixty years old. It had three wide drawers and two smaller drawers, side by side on top. All the drawers had button knobs, and the wood was dinged up and discolored with age. The dresser stood on four legs, leaving about nine inches of space between the bottom of the dresser and the floor. One of the legs had a large scratch in the wood. There were also a few large gashes on top, and from the condition of the surface, it looked as if it had been put in a shed or barn for a time and covered with heavier items. Being out in the elements would also explain the warping of the bottom drawer that caused it to stick.

Before working on the drawer, Elizabeth decided the best thing would be to wipe everything down. She noticed the dust from sanding and a few spiderwebs. She didn't want any creatures jumping out at her.

From the display area of the barn, Elizabeth could hear Mary's conversation with two women who were looking for Pyrex bowls, especially the Butterprint pattern. There was a lightness to Mary's voice that brought a sense of peace to Elizabeth's heart. After Mary's outburst last night, she'd been worried that her two younger sisters would start arguing again about who the quilt should go to. She chuckled to herself. After the last couple of months, she should have guessed that the challenge of a new mystery would prove irresistible to all three Classen sisters.

Elizabeth worked quickly with her rag, wiping down all the surfaces. She'd just finished when Martha arrived wearing an old painting shirt and carrying a paint can of primer and a brush. A drop cloth was tucked under her arm.

A twinge pricked at Elizabeth's heart seeing the old painting shirt. She recognized it as one of their father's shirts. It had been large even on him, and now it hung on Martha like a dress. Daddy had always worn it when doing painting projects, lest he face their mother's ire when he got paint on his "good" work clothes.

Martha spread out the drop cloth and then set the paint-brush down on the can. She glanced up and must have noticed the look in Elizabeth's eyes as she looked at the shirt.

Martha lifted one eyebrow. "I wondered if I should put it on," she finally admitted. "I think it would have brought a smile to Daddy's face to see me wearing it, but it does bring all kinds of ache too."

"Yes." Elizabeth sighed. "And isn't that what our life has become—the collecting and sharing of memories in numerous ways?" She swept her hand toward the front of the shop. "Isn't that why people come here? To find something similar to an item they remembered in their childhood? Or to find items that are reminiscent of days long past, simpler times, maybe?"

"I suppose I never thought of it that way before." Martha eased herself onto her knees in front of the dresser. "It's the same with the baked goods. I've had more than one person comment that my muffins and scones take them back to their childhood. Not like those too-sweet cake pops that are popular these days." She chuckled.

"Which makes me understand even more why both Anne and Betty are so eager to have the quilt for themselves. Obviously, the quilt can't belong to both families, but there was something about it that reminded them of a special time, a childhood memory, or of days long past when things were simpler...and maybe even happier."

Martha chuckled again, louder this time. "Listen to you! You're going to make me tear up." She pretended to wipe her eyes, then squatted and took hold of the right knob of the bottom drawer. "Here, help me finagle out this dresser drawer, will you?"

Elizabeth knelt beside her sister and took hold of the drawer's left knob. She started to pull on the knob, but it was loose. "I'm afraid if I pull too hard the knob is just going to come off. And then where will we be?"

Martha nodded. "My knob is firm, but I can't pull from just one side, or the drawer cocks sideways." She scratched her head. "Why don't you look underneath and see if there's something you can get ahold of to push or pull it out."

Elizabeth offered her a wry grin. "Hey, you're younger than I am. Shouldn't you be the one crawling around on the floor?" Still, she lay sideways, rested her head on the painter's cloth, and reached underneath the dresser. There was no bottom panel enclosing the chest, and the bottom of the drawer was rough and unfinished, snagging against the skin on her fingers. She rubbed along it, looking for something to hold on to, while at the same time also hoping she didn't get a splinter.

"I know," she mumbled, her face nearly pressing into one of the legs. "If I can get my fingers to the back, I can wedge them between the back of the drawer and the back panel and push the drawer forward."

"You can try it, but don't get your fingers stuck."

Elizabeth reached her fingers back, and sure enough, she found a space between the drawer and the panel. She squeezed in a few fingers and pulled the drawer toward her, wiggling it as she did. It took effort, but soon the drawer moved, and she heard something rustling inside, as if there was an old newspaper shuffling around.

"That's enough," Martha said. "I can pull it out the rest of the way. If you keep pushing it out, you're going to smack your head with the drawer."

"Well, I certainly don't want to do that." Elizabeth pulled her hand back, sat up, and brushed herself off the best she could. Then she watched as Martha eased the drawer out the rest of the way.

"I think I heard something crinkling in there—" Elizabeth started to say just as she was interrupted by her sister.

"Look. There's something in here."

Both sisters leaned over the drawer and noticed some folded papers resting in the back. Martha finished pulling the drawer out and then set it on the floor. After brushing the dust from her hands, she reached into the drawer and pulled the papers out. "I wonder how old these are. Looks like a piece of history, doesn't it?"

Martha moved from her knees to sitting on the floor and then unfolded the papers and shuffled through them. "There's a name on one of these..." Her eyes widened, and her jaw dropped. "Oh, Elizabeth. You're not going to believe this."

"What?" Elizabeth scooted over to her sister's side and then gasped as she read the name at the bottom of the page Elizabeth was holding. "A letter from Melinda Yoder? Of all things!"

Martha started to read the letter out loud, but Elizabeth reached out and stopped her. "Wait, Martha. Shouldn't we save this until Mary can be with us? It's only fair, I think."

Martha looked up. "Well...," she said reluctantly and then sighed. "I guess you're right. We'll read these the first chance we have when we're all together." She refolded the papers together, placed them on top of the dresser, opened the primer can, and picked up her paintbrush. "At least we know who Melinda Yoder is now. Just think, a few days ago we wouldn't have had any idea."

Footsteps sounded from behind Elizabeth, and she turned to see Mary approaching. "Hey, you two. I've got Angelina on hold. She wants to know if we can come tomorrow evening instead of today. She has a customer who needs her to go through his mother's things sooner rather than later. His mother's house was sold right before she passed away, so they need to get the house emptied as soon as possible. I can't even imagine how painful that would be."

Elizabeth waved a hand at her youngest sister. "I don't see any reason we can't change nights. Do you, Martha?"

Martha shook her head. "Sounds fine to me."

Mary started to turn, but paused, frowned, and sniffed a couple of times, then put her hand under her nose. "Martha, do you think you should be doing that now? Will the smell drive away our customers?"

"Oh no." Martha lowered her brush. "I didn't think of that." She reached for the can lid. "I'll put this back on and paint later. Hmm...maybe I'll have to paint it tonight and leave some of the windows open to give the place time to air out."

"That sounds like a plan. Thank you," Mary said. "Now, I really must get back to Angelina and tell her we'll see her tomorrow night." She turned and went back to the shop before Elizabeth could share their discovery with her.

As Martha put the lid back on her paint can, Elizabeth couldn't resist peeking through the papers. As she fanned the top edges, she saw that they were all letters, none of them with the same handwriting, and they were written on various types of paper. She was looking closer at one of them when she heard Martha clear her throat. She looked up guiltily to Martha's raised eyebrows. "I see you're not so worried about being fair to Mary, now that *you're* the one holding the papers."

Elizabeth felt her face flush. "I must admit, the view is a little different from this perspective, yes." She put the folded papers in her apron pocket and held up three fingers in the Girl Scout salute. "I promise I'll wait until we can all look."

Martha laughed. "A lot of good that does us. You were never a Girl Scout."

Elizabeth grinned at her. "No. But since I figure you won't let me out of your sight until we read the letters together, it doesn't make a whole lot of difference."

"Very true, dear sister. You know me well." Martha linked elbows with Elizabeth. "Now why don't you help Mary with the teeming crowds while I get changed and check the display case." She tapped her finger under her eye. "And remember, I'll have my eye on you."

CHAPTER NINE

A s the three sisters sipped frosty glasses of lemonade at the kitchen table, Martha unfolded the letters and spread them out. Along the top of each letter was written something else in various handwriting: *The 1907 Girls.*

Mary pointed to the top of the letters. "What do you think that means, 'The 1907 Girls'?"

Martha picked up a letter—the one with Melinda's name at the top. "My guess is that this was a circle letter group for girls in this community born in 1907. That would make them about thirteen years old at the time of these letters, since it appears many of these were written in 1920."

Mary picked up another letter. "This one is from a girl named Irma—oh, that must be Anne's cousin. It's dated March 13, 1920. Listen to this— '*Yesterday* Daed *woke me early. He said our pig was birthing, and he knew I'd want to be there. Last year I helped care for the runt, and guess what I have in my lap now? Daed showed me how to dip my finger in milk and put it in the pig's mouth. It made me giggle. The suction is strong for one so young.*'" Mary sighed. "It's so sweet."

Excitement built in Martha's chest at the realization they'd just discovered a piece of history. "1920. I wish I knew more about what was happening during that time." She stroked her chin. "If I'm figuring right, it had only been eight years since the sinking of the *Titanic,* and World War I had just ended a couple of years earlier, although I'm not sure how either event would have impacted Pennsylvania Amish girls."

Mary scanned the letter she was holding. "That's true. Listen to this, from Melinda." She cleared her throat and then read. "'*I dared to complain to* Maam *today about having to weed the garden. Oh, the look on her face. Not of anger. Ne, disappointment. I went back to my work, ashamed of my words, when Maam came to me. She told me that she had not liked weeding much when she was a girl, yet her daed told her that she should be proud to do God's work. She said that gardening was the most essential job on earth. What other work allows you to see God's creation so close and work along His side? I suppose I had never thought of such a thing before.'*"

Mary's voice was low as she read, and amazement shone in her eyes. "Can you imagine thirteen-year-old girls talking about such things today? Boys, celebrities, clothes, music. Then there is all the bullying. I'm thankful to have raised my kids when I did. It seems kids now are trying to grow up so quickly. And they're so busy texting each other. I can't imagine a thirteen-year-old sitting down to write a real pen-to-paper letter." She placed the letter she'd been holding on the table and smoothed it with her hands. "I can't imagine one teen girl writing such a letter to friends, let alone a whole group of them."

Martha frowned. "I think you're being too hard on today's teenage girls, Mary. I'm sure there are plenty who don't think beyond the shallow stuff you mentioned, but I also think there are young girls who are serious minded and concerned about their education, their futures, and how they can make the world better."

"Mary..." Elizabeth interrupted the sisters' disagreement. "Why don't you read another letter? We have quite a few to get through."

Mary did as she was told and read. The next letter was from Katie, expressing excitement about spring, their new baby calves, and the names of all the barn cats. The letter seemed to be from someone younger than thirteen in some ways, yet Martha figured that was because it was a simpler, more innocent time. She selected another letter—"This one is dated April 4, 1920, and is from Pearl"—and began reading.

"*Dear Friends, I regret I did not write you sooner, but I was taken ill. That kept me from answering your interesting letters, and I am sorry the letters stopped with me for a time. Many of us here got the fever, but I got it worse. My little* bruder *had a cough with it. Maam was not getting much sleep so I took Jacob for the night. I did not tell Maam that Jacob slept like an angel for me. It truly was no sacrifice at all.*

"*We are all doing better now, and I am thankful for the sun outside the window. The chill of the winter was making me as gray as the clouds above. Hopefully the last of the snow is melted. At least there was no more sloshing through wet, dirty snow to go to* schul, *now that that's through*—'"

"What does she mean, school is through? Did they really get out in April back then?" Mary interrupted.

"Oh, no," Elizabeth explained. "I think she means she was completely done with school. Remember, Amish children only go through the eighth grade."

Martha skimmed the rest of the letter about Pearl's daily experiences. Nothing she read seemed to be important, until she got to the very last paragraph.

"Wait, listen to this," she said, her voice rising with excitement. "*I know we might not have much free time, except for in the evenings after chores are done, but what if we did something together. Wouldn't it be wonderful to*—'"

"And?" Mary asked, tapping her fingers on the tabletop. "Go on. What was her idea? What would be wonderful?"

Martha returned the letter to the table and shrugged. "I'm not sure. The letter ends there. She must have continued on another page—one that was lost."

"Lost?" Mary gasped. "Out of all the letters to lose, why that one?"

"Do you think they were talking about making a quilt together?" Elizabeth wondered aloud.

Martha lifted her glass of lemonade and took a sip. "It could be possible," she said over the rim. "Hattie certainly thought that could happen."

Mary lifted her own glass. "Yes, and that could be why it appears some of the squares were made by different people, especially when it comes to the shapes of the letters and the stitching. Some of the squares seem better stitched than others—"

"Yet still there is no proof," Elizabeth interrupted. "We could be reading into the letters what we want them to say. There are any number of things she could be about to suggest they make together. Maybe Betty would be able to give us more insight."

Martha reached for another letter, deciding to read them all a few times to see if there were any more clues, but Elizabeth was right. They were probably reading more into these letters than was there out of their desire to solve their own mystery. The point of these letters was simply for the girls to share friendship, not to point the way for amateur detectives a century later. Still, if she had to read through something, these were delightful. And she had a feeling Betty would enjoy reading them too. And maybe, just maybe, reading her aunt's letter would spur another memory of the quilt.

CHAPTER TEN

"Maybe today we'll solve the riddle of the quilt," Martha said as she parked in front of the large warehouse. Angelina also had a storefront in town, but she'd told them the items they were most interested in would be here. The warehouse used to be an old dairy. Large maples waved leaves in a greeting. Across a small pasture, a large silver silo jutted into the sky. Martha remembered driving by this dairy as a young girl and seeing these fields dotted with cows. Things changed over time, even in rural Pennsylvania.

"I called Betty this morning," Mary said as she got out of the car. "I left a message on her answering machine, telling her about the letters, but she hasn't called me back yet."

"And I called Anne," said Martha. She got out of the car and waited to lock the doors until her sisters were unloaded and on the sidewalk. "She said she has company at her house for a couple of days, but as soon as they leave she'll call, and we'll get together so she can see the letters."

Angelina must have been waiting for them, because the door of the warehouse opened, and she stepped out into the summer breeze. Martha smiled at her. "Angelina, it's so nice to see you again," she called as she approached. "Thank you for taking time in your evening to meet with us."

"I'm happy to help you." Angelina held the door and motioned for them to come inside. "But explain to me what this is for again?"

"It's about a quilt," Elizabeth cut in, stepping forward. "There was a quilt in the last bunch of things we purchased from you." She released a long sigh. "We put it out for display, and within two days two people wanted to buy it."

Angelina tilted her head and looked from Elizabeth to Mary to Martha. Her furrowed brow proved she was still confused. "And that's a problem because...?"

Martha explained. "It's a problem because both women claim a family member quilted it. They remember it being in a relative's home growing up. Neither will back down on her story."

Angelina's shoulders eased. "It's obvious someone's mistaken." A breeze picked up and blew long strands of blond hair across her face. "You wouldn't happen to have the quilt with you, would you?"

Martha looked at Mary. "Did we bring it?"

Mary's jaw dropped. "I thought you were going to—"

"Yes, we have it." Elizabeth hurried to the car. "I put it in the trunk earlier in the day so we wouldn't forget."

As Angelina, Martha, and Mary stepped inside the warehouse, Elizabeth went back to the car, opened the driver's door, and popped the trunk. Then she retrieved the quilt and joined the other women in the warehouse. She also carried a bakery bag tied with ribbon. She entered and shut the door behind her and extended the bag to Angelina. "Thank you for helping us today. Martha makes the most wonderful strawberry cream cheese muffins. I thought you'd enjoy these."

Angelina's face softened. "Oh, thank you. I really do appreciate it." She took the bag from Elizabeth. Then she pointed to a long worktable. "We can lay the quilt out over there. I have so many things going through my hands. It's hard for me to remember everything, but I do have a copy of the receipt and the estate this quilt came from." She moved to a filing cabinet. "Secondhand Blessings, correct?"

"That's us," Mary said.

Elizabeth moved toward the table, and Martha helped her remove the quilt from its protective bag. As they laid out the quilt, Martha studied it again.

"Knowing where the quilt came from would help." Martha smoothed her fingers over it.

Angelina searched through the middle drawer of the cabinet and then pulled out a file. "Oh good. I found it. I'm behind on my filing, and I'm so glad..." She turned and paused midsentence. "Oh no! That's the quilt?" Angelina rushed forward.

"Yes. It's the quilt."

Angelina placed the unopened file on top of the quilt and then placed her hands on her hips and shook her head. "Then we have a problem. A big, big problem."

Martha's heartbeat quickened in her chest. "What do you mean?"

"If I remember correctly, this quilt is a family heirloom. It wasn't supposed to be sold. It must have accidentally been put into the sell pile instead of the keep pile."

"Are you kidding me?" Elizabeth's voice shot out. "We have two people fighting over this quilt, and it wasn't even supposed to be sold in the first place?"

"Wait." Martha held her hands in the air. "Are you *sure* this is the same quilt? Maybe you should look in the file to be sure."

Angelina nodded, but the color had drained from her face. "I'll look, but I have a feeling this quilt got put in the wrong pile." She opened the file. "I see here that I consigned a tin washtub, some framed prints, a dresser, stoneware, and a quilt." She narrowed her gaze and looked closer. "My notes say, 'Homemade quilt. Red, blue, green. Looks unique. Owner did not believe it was a family heirloom." Relief flooded Angelina's face. "Oh good. I'm so thankful I wrote that note. I suppose...I suppose it was all right I sold it."

Elizabeth pretended to wipe her brow. "Whew. For a second I thought all this fight was about a quilt we weren't even allowed to sell in the first place."

Angelina continued to study the list. "Yes, I suppose I was mistaken...but I have to say that in most cases a handmade quilt like this one wouldn't be part of an estate sale. It's really unusual—"

"Unless it didn't belong to the family," Mary cut in. "Then it would make sense."

Martha pointed at the file cabinet. "Can you tell us whose estate the quilt came from?"

"Most people aren't too concerned about me sharing that information. It's a small community. Everyone knows everyone, but let me go look up this reference number. All the release forms will be there." Angelina moved to the file cabinet, opening a different drawer this time. The three sisters watched, anxiously.

Martha felt the excitement in each sister on both sides. "I cannot believe how such a little thing can turn into such a big deal." She sighed. "Just think, if Anne would have just bought the quilt that first day, we wouldn't be doing any of this."

"That's true," Mary said. "But at least—maybe by the end of this—we'll know who the rightful owner is."

Angelina read her file and then returned it to the drawer. "I'm sorry. It's very unusual, but the family didn't sign the release form. There is a note that says I am not to disclose where these items came from."

Martha studied the quilt for a moment, and part of her wanted to just flip a coin and sell it to the winner. They already had plenty to do, running Secondhand Blessings. How much time could they give something like this? Yet something deep within her knew that if she gave up now she'd always wonder about the truth, and she knew her sisters would too.

"What's next?" Mary looked from Martha to Elizabeth.

"That's a good question." Martha turned to Angelina. "I know you can't tell us where the items came from, but can we look at the other items that came in the same lot? The ones you didn't consign to us?"

Angelina nodded. "Yes, of course. I mean that's my job, buying and selling. So if you are interested in making more purchases, I'd be happy to show you what I have."

She moved toward a line of stalls. At one time, they'd been used to separate cows, but as Martha walked by each, she saw that they now held piles and stacks of various items. The sounds of their shoes on the concrete filled the room.

"I used to have one large warehouse, and I'd throw everything together as soon as I purchased it," Angelina explained, "but it became so confusing."

"What do you mean?" Martha asked.

"Estate sales are hard on the family. Usually by the time I've arrived they have had a chance to go through their loved ones' things. They pick items they each want, and when I arrive, I take the rest. I've discovered I can get a better deal if I take everything left over. But there have been cases where a family member comes later, asking for a specific item. I've learned to hang on to each family's items and keep them separate from other families' things for at least several weeks or longer. Then it's easy for a family member to find what they're looking for."

"And it makes it easier for us," Mary said. "I'm curious now what else was in the lot."

"We all are." Elizabeth stopped to look into one of the stalls.

Angelina led them to the end of the aisle. "All the items from that estate sale are in this stall. I should have a delivery arriving any minute, so if you don't mind—"

"Don't feel you have to babysit us." Mary smiled as if to put the woman's mind at ease. "We'll do some sleuthing, but I also believe we'll be doing some buying." She chuckled as she pointed to Elizabeth. "In fact, someone has her eye on that infant's gown."

"Oh yes." Elizabeth clasped her hands. "Can't you picture it framed and on a wall of a nursery? It looks handmade..."

"And it looks old," Martha commented. "Yet another item that most families wouldn't get rid of, especially not in an estate sale."

Angelina tilted her head. "I think I heard the delivery truck. I'll help Samuel unload, but let me know if you need his help. There are some heavy boxes and chests. He might need to move them for you."

Martha nodded. "Thank you. My sisters and I appreciate this." She scanned the stall and lifted an eyebrow. "And I have a feeling this might work out for you as well. We always appreciate the items you bring, and I bet we'll return to our store with our car full."

Angelina moved to open the door to the unloading dock. "Perfect. Exactly what I want to hear," she called over her shoulder.

"Well, this isn't how I imagined spending my evening," Martha said, sighing as Angelina disappeared from sight, "but I know one thing right off the bat."

"What's that?" Elizabeth asked.

"We're gonna need a bigger car."

CHAPTER ELEVEN

On Sunday morning Martha didn't need Reddy to rouse her from her bed. By the time he sounded his first raucous cry, she was in the kitchen cooking breakfast. Yesterday's trip to the warehouse hadn't been quite distracting enough to keep her from waking at 3 a.m. with the question she'd had on her heart for the past two years. Why would God take Chuck without even letting her say goodbye to him or tell him she loved him one last time? Would she ever get past this feeling, like there was something left undone, this feeling of something unfulfilled?

Elizabeth ambled into the kitchen, yawning. "What are you doing up so early? Are those blueberry pancakes I smell?"

Martha picked up her spatula to flip a pancake and skipped over Elizabeth's first question, hoping her sister wouldn't notice. "Yup. With a little extra vanilla, just the way you like 'em."

"Yum." Elizabeth poured herself a cup of coffee and sat at the table. "If I haven't said it lately, I sure appreciate all you do around here. I never ate like this before you came."

Martha put two pancakes on a plate and handed it to Elizabeth, then passed the butter to her. "You know I love cooking for more than just myself. And coming home to this place has been the best decision I've made in a long time." She spooned more batter into the frying pan.

Elizabeth poured syrup on her pancakes. "Remind me to get another bottle of this from the shop sometime. Nobody cooks down maple sap like Silas Fischer." She took a bite then wiped her mouth with her napkin. "If I remember right, we're coming up on the anniversary of when we lost Chuck, aren't we?"

Martha's heart warmed, hearing Elizabeth include herself in missing Chuck. "We are. A week from tomorrow, actually."

She was grateful when Elizabeth continued eating, not trying to fill the silence and Martha's sadness with reassuring chatter.

Elizabeth finished her pancakes and stood to put her plate in the sink. "We could do something special that day," she said. "Maybe expressing gratitude for his life can help us fill the vacuum he left behind. If there's something that would mean a lot to you, be sure to tell me. You're my little sister, and I want to do what I can to help."

She gave Martha a hug and left to get ready for church. Martha finished making the rest of the pancakes and put them in the oven to keep warm until Mary came down for breakfast. As she ran water over the frying pan, she reflected on what Elizabeth had said. Was gratitude an antidote for this feeling of something left undone? Would being deliberately and specifically grateful help her accept the brutal suddenness of her loss? "Well," she said to herself as she climbed the stairs to her room, "there's only one way to find out."

CHAPTER TWELVE

The sisters had only stayed an hour or so on Saturday at Angelina's and had indeed filled up all the free space in the car for items they wanted to consign. Martha had done her chores and was waiting by the car on Monday morning, watching for Mary. Elizabeth had offered to stay at Secondhand Blessings while the other two went back to the warehouse to sort through the last of the things from the estate sale. She had a twinkle in her eye as they left.

"And Mary, if you need any help, ask Samuel. He seemed extra eager to help you move items last night—and promised to be there today."

Mary laughed. "I'll keep that in mind. He was kinda cute."

Martha snorted. "First it's Bill. Then it's Rafe Porter. Now it's Samuel? Good grief, Mary. I can't keep up with you. Didn't you tell Bill you were ready to date?"

Mary opened her car door. "I told him I was ready to date. I didn't tell him I was ready to date just *him*." She put her hand on her hip. "There's no reason for Bill to be hurt if I don't tie myself down just yet."

"Hmm, even if he is, doesn't love heal all wounds? I think I've heard that before," Elizabeth said with a wave.

Those words stayed on Martha's mind as she drove to the old dairy. She'd had to adjust to a new way of driving since she'd moved back to Bird-in-Hand. You never knew when you'd turn a corner and happen on a slow-moving buggy. *Opposites sure do attract,* she thought. Chuck had been a slow, deliberate driver. Martha smiled as she remembered how she used to beg him to at least go the speed limit, and how he used to feign fear and grab the dash during some of her faster maneuvers. He always, without fail, came to a complete stop at all stop signs, while Martha mostly thought it was good enough to do more than a yield but not quite a stop through the ones on empty country roads. She'd gotten a good laugh once when they were riding in his pickup through a neighbor's field, and he flashed his turn signal before turning left. Martha had teased him for days afterward, wondering if the cows appreciated his thoughtfulness.

Lord, thank You that Chuck was a steady man I could depend on, who kept me and the children safe.

They passed the Grabers' house on the left, and Martha waved to Lucille, who was hanging laundry with her youngest daughter, Rose. Martha made a mental note to tell Lucille they were running low on the honey she and her two older daughters sold in Secondhand Blessings. She'd forgotten to tell her at church yesterday.

Martha's thoughts drifted to Elizabeth's words from just a few minutes ago, and she glanced over at the passenger seat. "Mary?" she asked.

"Hmm?" Mary seemed lost in her own thoughts.

"Do you think that what Elizabeth said is true, that love heals all wounds?"

Mary shrugged. "I don't know. Yes, I suppose so." She nibbled on her lower lip. "I believe love has been healing me after my divorce. Love from my sisters and love from God. Why do you ask?"

"I don't know. I've just been thinking about it. We've been so busy trying to decide who should get the quilt that maybe we've missed the bigger picture."

"What do you mean?"

Martha turned down the country road toward the dairy, taking in the beauty of the countryside, dressed in summer's finest.

"We've been so concerned about finding out if the quilt should go to Anne—or go to Betty. But maybe all this has happened to bring them together. Wasn't it Rachel who said that they used to be good friends until Anne left the Amish?"

Mary frowned. "You're not thinking about asking them to share the quilt, are you?"

"No, but something deep down tells me that all this is happening for a reason. If love heals all wounds, maybe this quilt can be used to mend their friendship. Maybe God is letting this happen for a reason."

Mary laughed. "Oh sure, trying to solve a mystery isn't enough for you. Now you're hoping for a miracle."

Martha parked her car in front of the dairy. "I'm not hoping for a miracle...I just have a feeling that somehow God is going to use all of this for good."

Mary opened her car door, and the scent of rain drifted in. "I'd like to see that too." There was a wistfulness in her voice. "The healing of hearts...yes, that is God's work, isn't it?"

They closed the car doors and then walked side by side toward the warehouse area. The door opened, but it was Samuel, not Angelina, who opened the door.

"There you are." He looked first at Mary and then at Martha. "I have good news."

Martha tilted her head as she followed Mary into the warehouse. "Good news?"

Samuel closed the door behind them and then paused. He hooked his thumbs in the belt loops of his jeans. He was of average height and slim—a clean-cut sort of guy. In her younger years, Mary had always gone for the edgier, more reckless men, which ended up getting her into trouble by marrying the wrong type of person. Samuel seemed like a nice enough guy—someone Mary might enjoy spending time with.

Samuel ran his fingers through his dark hair, streaked with gray. "Yes, Angelina checked the records again last night, and she discovered there is a second stall that has items from the estate sale you're interested in."

Mary's shoulders sank. "A second stall? That'll be even more work. It's going to take us all day."

Samuel had a sheepish look on his face. "Actually, I got here early and already did a lot of the sorting. I could tell last night that you were looking mostly for old books or papers that might have information about the person the quilt belonged to. So I put everything I thought you might find helpful into a pile."

Martha's heart warmed at the gesture.

Mary smiled at him. "Wow, that was really thoughtful of you. Thank you."

"Yes, that will save us a lot of time," Martha added. "Will you be able to stay...?" She glanced at Mary. "Uh, just in case we need more help?"

"I have to make a delivery. There's a store in Bird-in-Hand that's bought a number of pieces. But I might be back before you leave." His eyes looked hopeful.

Martha straightened her shoulders. She resisted the urge to look at Mary and wink. "We appreciate your help and would be glad to see you when you return if we're still here."

"Wonderful." Samuel's smile was wide as he removed a large-brimmed hat off a hat rack by the door. "I hope to see you later then." He moved to the door and paused. "The items I've sorted are in the stall across from the one you searched last night."

"Again, that was so kind of you, Samuel." Martha followed him to the door. "You've saved us hours of work, and it's appreciated."

Samuel left, and the rumble of his truck filled the air as he drove away. The sisters were silent as they walked to the stalls. They found the one he mentioned without a problem. Martha nearly skipped as she noticed boxes filled with items that seemed more personal in nature—surely those items would have more information about the owner of the quilt and would possibly give them an idea of who the quilt had belonged to.

Two folding chairs had been set up in front of the boxes. Martha sat with a smile. "My goodness, but Samuel thought of everything, didn't he?"

Mary sat down too. "Yes, he is a very nice man. I hope we're still here when he returns."

Martha chuckled. "Oh, I bet you do."

Mary eyed her sister, and Martha hurried on to say, "Of course, you hardly know him. You'd have to build a friendship with him first."

"Wait a minute." Mary lifted her hand, pausing her sister's words. "Is my big sister getting all protective and trying to tell me how to date a guy?"

Martha stared at her. "Mary, don't tell me you'd go on a date by yourself with a man you've only just met and know nothing about. Don't you know what could happen?" She counted off on her fingers. "He could be a serial killer. He could be a con man. He could be a fugitive. He could be a drifter. He could be a bigamist. How would you know?"

Mary frowned at her. "Are you saying I'm not smart enough to know how to tell if a man is good or evil? Are you saying I need to run any guy by you before I can date him? That you need to interrogate him for me? Maybe you'd like to run a background check?" By the end of her speech, her cheeks were as bright as her pink sweater.

Martha held up her hands. "Whoa, calm down, little sis. I didn't mean any of those things. I just don't think you should take every man at his word that he's a nice guy. By the time you find out he's not telling the truth, it could be too late." She grinned. "And yes. I want to interrogate every man who asks you out. Is that too much for a big sister to ask?"

Mary glared at her, then burst out laughing. "I'm going to ignore that, *big* sis, and address your real concern. If Samuel asks me out, I'll make sure for our first date that I meet him in a very public place. The second date, if there is another one, I'll ask him to dinner at our house. *If* he asks me out. Deal?"

Martha held out her hand. "Deal," she said, as Mary shook it. They grinned at each other. "Now, let's get to work."

Piece by piece, they went through all the papers in the boxes Samuel had set aside for them. They not only didn't find anything important, they also didn't find anything that could give them information about the family the belongings came from. Instead, it was just a collection of old *HomeLife* magazines, which were popular among the Amish, and some sketches that seemed to be done by a child's hand.

Mary brushed her hand across her forehead, leaving a smudge of dirt. "Looks like we've gone through everything. It's a shame we spent all this time and didn't discover anything worthwhile."

"Wait a minute." Martha stood and moved past the boxes. "What about this?" She pointed to an old blanket. Something was peeking out from underneath. She pushed the blanket to the side. Underneath was a charming, though battered, writing desk. "We didn't go through this."

She opened it carefully, and her breath caught as she did. "Oh, Mary, look!"

There, in the desk, was a stack of papers—just like the ones they'd found in the old dresser. "Look, Mary...more circle letters!"

"Do you think different girls made the blocks and sent them to Melinda, and she made the quilt?"

Martha gingerly picked up the letters. "Or maybe they worked on it together—like in a sewing circle and then—"

"Maybe they *shared* the quilt?" Mary suggested. "That would explain why both women remember it. Maybe they passed it around."

"Let's read these letters and see if we can learn anything more." Martha couldn't help but smile. "Guessing won't do anyone any good."

"Yes, but we better read them here." Mary glanced around as if looking for someone. "We can't just take them."

"You're right. We could only take them if we asked Angelina."

Mary glanced at her watch. "It's nearly lunchtime. Shouldn't it be time for Samuel to return?"

Martha tilted her head, listening for his truck. "I don't know. I wasn't paying attention."

It wasn't ten minutes later when Martha heard Samuel's truck. His whistle preceded him down the hall. He approached with a smile on his face and a large paper bag in his hand. A logo on the side of the bag read THE VILLAGE BAKERY.

Samuel held up the bag for them to see. "I brought us lunch. As a bachelor, I've learned about the best deals. The Village Bakery has a punch card, and on Monday it's double punch."

"Let us pay you," Mary said.

He waved a hand toward them. "No need. I got three punches today—one for each sandwich. I have enough for a free sandwich now."

"Wonderful. That's very kind of you."

He'd gotten them all chicken salad sandwiches. Martha took a large bite. It was delicious—the best chicken salad she'd had in a while.

The three of them chatted about their memories growing up in the area, but all too soon, Samuel had to leave. "I have more deliveries. I need to get them done. I promised my maam

I'd chop some wood for her. She's certain we'll get a bad storm next week. Says her bones are aching something fierce."

Mary eyed Samuel curiously. "You said *maam*. Are you Amish?"

He seemed surprised. "My parents used to be when I was young. Now they're Mennonite. I attend the same church they do, but my hair doesn't look good in that straight-across cut." He chuckled. "Call me vain."

Martha couldn't help but laugh. "I hope you can get everything done in time. And maybe we'll see you again. Especially if we need any deliveries made to Secondhand Blessings."

Samuel nodded as he stood. "It sounds like a plan." He pointed to the letters. "And I hope you'll find what you need in those."

"Thank you, Samuel." Mary picked a letter up. "I hope so too."

Angelina arrived as they were looking at the letters more closely. The first thing Martha checked to see was if they were written by the same group of girls as the letters they'd already read. They were. Martha smiled to see Melinda's name among the letter writers.

"I was hoping you'd still be here," Angelina said, handing over two cups of coffee. "It's nothing fancy, just black, but I thought you might need a pick-me-up. Sorting through this much stuff can get tiring."

"To tell you the truth, I've been so intent on our search I didn't even consider if I was getting worn out. Samuel brought us lunch, which was sweet of him and gave us a break." Martha took a sip of her coffee. "You don't mind if we read these letters, do you?"

"Not at all." Angelina tucked a strand of long blond hair behind her ear. "If you need me, I'll be in the office going over paperwork." She sighed. "There seems to never be an end to paperwork."

Angelina had started to walk away when Mary called out to her, "Can we buy these letters from you? I'd hate to see them not appreciated. If they are what we think they are."

"Actually, you can have them. They are of no use to me."

"Thank you," Martha called. "It doesn't seem right," she told Mary once Angelina was out of earshot. "Some memories are treasured, and others are treated as trash."

CHAPTER THIRTEEN

Martha and Mary sat side by side on the folding chairs as they read through the letters, sunlight seeping through the slats of the former dairy's ceiling.

Martha came to a passage she wanted to share. "Listen to this from a girl named Hazel King, from May 1922." She began to read it aloud.

"*Today* Grossmammi *asked me to sit in the sewing circle with her, my aenti, and my maam. I saw the worry on Maam's face. She has seen my stitching, but Grossmammi has not. Maam's stitches are neat and small, mine are large and uneven. If Grossmammi knew, she would not have invited me.*

"*I offered to make lunch for everyone there, and that pleased Grossmammi even more. The last time she visited she complimented my pie. Pie is easy to make. It takes no small stitching. I'd rather make pie any day.*

"*Why does quilting have to be so hard? No matter how hard I try, I cannot create neat and tiny stitches like Maam's. I was almost worried to send any of my stitching to you, but since so many of you have fretted about your own stitching I knew I could console you with my efforts.*'"

Martha thought about what it might have been like back then for these girls. "As much as I sometimes envy the Amish their simple lifestyle and strong family ties, I have to remember that it's not always easy for them. The young women are pretty limited in their choices, and all of them must learn to sew, to cook everything from scratch, to can the food from their gardens, to raise children, and take care of their elderly parents."

Mary looked up from the letter in her hand. "And some of them must long for more education than they're allowed."

"Yes, I suppose you're right." Martha continued reading the letters to herself, and the minutes slipped away as she read about the lives of these lively young Amish women from the 1920s.

"Listen to this." Martha held up another letter, eager for Mary to hear. "This is from Melinda, Betty's aunt."

Mary turned to her, eyes intent as Martha read the letter to her.

"'*Monday, laundry day, brought rain. Instead of hanging the clothes on the line, Daed strung the lines in the front room. My younger bruders and* schwesders *danced under the clothes and laughed when water dripped on them. I watched from the corner chair as I worked on my sampler. Maam says I must finish my sampler before I can start on my quilt squares, but she approves of our idea.*

"'*I also know one of the verses I would like to stitch: "The things which are not seen are eternal." 2 Corinthians 4:18. I memorized the whole verse at schul. I hope to do my best, though I have to admit my stitching is not very neat. At least I am not the only one. I have not heard about which scriptures each of you are stitching, except Katie, who said she has chosen Proverbs 3:5. My hope is that if I get this letter off soon that the next envelope I receive will include a quilt square or two—*'"

"Oh, Martha!" Mary's words interrupted her reading. "That letter proves it. We *are* onto something. The girls were making quilt squares. Most likely the squares from the very quilt we have back at the house."

Martha felt a lump of emotion in her throat. "We haven't figured out who the quilt belongs to, but at least we've found a bit of the history." She pulled another letter from the stack. In her mind, she again pictured the young Amish girls. It was almost as if these letters had opened a window in time. She sucked in her breath. "Oh, I know what we can do with the letters."

"What do you mean?" Mary asked.

"We know two of the family members of these girls—Anne and Betty. Since they care about the quilt so much, they will appreciate reading the letters." She smiled. "And we don't have to worry about them fighting over them. We can give Betty's aunt's letters to her and Anne's cousin's letters to her."

"Yes, it sounds like a plan, but what if they find some way to fight about that too?"

"Surely they can't fight about letters that belong to the other's relative."

Mary rose and rubbed her arms. "I'm getting a little cross-eyed from all these letters. Angelina said we can have them. There's no need to sit here and read them." She slipped her purse over her shoulder. "We can take them home and read them tonight. It's probably not a bad idea to check on Elizabeth too. I'd like to think she would call us if things got too busy for her at the shop. But you know Elizabeth. Sometimes she sacrifices so we can enjoy ourselves."

The two sisters gathered their things and then straightened up everything they'd gone through, as best they could.

They were nearly finished when Angelina approached again. "Mary, Martha, I was going to tell you there are a few things I don't want. They are worth fixing up, but I don't have time." She pointed to a bookshelf that appeared to have been painted too many times. She also pointed to the small writing desk—the one they'd found the letters inside. "Even though I like the look of both, I don't want to tackle these projects now. Would you like them?"

Martha stepped closer to the writing desk. "I love this small piece. It's dinged up, but so precious." She smoothed her hair back from her face and then looked at Mary. "One of the girls might have written her letters on this very desk."

Mary eyed the bookshelf. "I like the look of the shelf too." She sighed. "But neither will fit in our car. Do you think Samuel could deliver them?"

"Of course." Angelina pulled her cell phone from her back pocket. "I'll send him a text right now. I'm not sure he'll be able to do it today. But maybe tomorrow."

Mary looked at Martha, wide-eyed with innocence, and Martha grinned in spite of herself. She knew her little sister. It might not be too long before they would be entertaining a new guest at their supper table.

CHAPTER FOURTEEN

Elizabeth rushed to the door as soon as she saw her sisters enter the shop. Her stomach rumbled, even though she'd already eaten three muffins. She should have brought a lunch out to Secondhand Blessings with her. The store had been busy all day, and she eagerly waited for her sisters to return so she could take a break and get a more substantial lunch than muffins. But before that she wanted to talk to them. Had it been worth it, going back to the warehouse? She had news to share with them too.

Thankfully, most of their customers had left. Only a few women looked through racks of clothes, picking out items to use for a fall theater production of *Our Town*. They chatted as they looked through vintage dresses, aprons, and suits, clearly having a good time browsing together.

Her sisters were both talking as they walked toward Elizabeth. "Remember Samuel, Angelina's delivery driver?" Martha started, struggling to catch her breath.

But before Martha could finish her sentence, a pink-cheeked Mary cut in. "Oh, Martha, we can talk about that later. Tell her about the letters!"

"Right." Martha held up a brown paper bag. "It's filled with letters—similar to the ones we found in the dresser." Elizabeth's eyes sparkled. "They're from the same group of girls!"

Mary added, "We read through a few of them, but we decided to wait and read the rest together."

Elizabeth took the bag from her sister, excited about this find. "Do they provide any more information about the quilt? Did you find any clues about who made it, or who it belongs to?" She hoped beyond hope that anything they found would point to the real owner.

"Yes to your first question...and we're still uncertain about the answer to the second." Mary crossed her arms. Her cheeks were still flushed, and Elizabeth didn't know if it was because of talk of Samuel or the excitement of finding the letters.

Elizabeth tucked the bag under her arm. "So the information you found won't help us know who the quilt belongs to?"

Martha shrugged. "We have a hint of who made it. What we read so far indicates the girls were working on quilt squares together. But who put it together and kept it, we don't know. We still have no idea who it belongs to."

"Well, at least we have something to keep us occupied. These letters should be interesting." Elizabeth set the letters on the counter and turned back to them. "But I have something to share with you too." She waited until both sets of eyes were turned to her before she began. "Betty called. She told me she talked to her cousin, Abigail, Melinda's daughter, and asked her about the quilt. Abigail said that her mother had many quilts, of course, but she didn't recall one like the one Betty was asking about. But then she said if Betty wanted to know more about Melinda's life growing up that she had something that might help. Abigail said that about forty years ago some researchers came to Lancaster County, wanting to record the memories and history of the Amish families and to preserve the Pennsylvania Dutch dialect. Melinda's family was interviewed, all of them, including the children."

"But how could they do that?" Martha asked. "The Amish don't allow their pictures to be taken. Isn't this the same thing?"

Elizabeth shook her head. "Abigail said the church elders debated for days about whether they should allow this, but finally decided that if the researchers would sign a contract that forbid them from ever selling or profiting off the recordings, and if the members themselves never possessed copies of the recordings, then it would be all right for their people to participate."

Excitement was evident on Martha's face, but Mary wore a more worried expression. "But if the interviews are in Pennsylvania Dutch, how are we going to understand them? Last I checked, neither of you spoke Amish."

Elizabeth smiled. "We don't have to. Abigail said that although the participants couldn't have the taped recordings of their interviews, the researchers gave them transcripts of them. Melinda translated hers into English and gave each of her children a copy of it in her own handwriting. Abigail brought her copy to Betty, and Betty is going to bring it to us this afternoon." She looked around the shop. "But in the meantime, I think we need to remember we have a shop to run. Martha, if you could get your display case refilled, that would be great. And Mary, I see some customers who look like they might appreciate your help. I'm going to go wolf down a sandwich, and I'll be right back."

On her way out of the shop, Elizabeth saw a car drive up with Betty in the passenger seat. When the driver parked, Betty opened her window and waved Elizabeth over to the car. When Elizabeth reached her, Betty handed her a large manila envelope. "I had Abigail make a copy for you, so you don't have to return this. The whole transcript isn't there—just the part where she talks about the quilt. I think there's proof in there that Melinda made the quilt, so I'm expecting to take it home very soon. Anne Hostetler will have to finally admit that it rightfully belongs to me."

She waved goodbye, rolled up the window, and the car took off down the driveway. Elizabeth retraced her steps to the shop and then to the display case. She showed the envelope in her hand to Martha, who gave her a thumbs-up and said, "Some light after-dinner reading for us, huh?"

Elizabeth groaned. "I knew you'd make me wait for you and Mary." Then she smirked and lifted her hand, three fingers up. "Do you need my Girl Scout promise again?"

Martha grinned back at her. "No, I trust you."

On her way to the house, Elizabeth breathed a prayer that between the letters and Melinda's interview, they could find some answers to their little mystery. Because it was becoming more and more obvious that it was something much more than that to Betty Yoder.

CHAPTER FIFTEEN

Martha made herself a cup of herbal tea with honey and then set the teacup on the side table before sitting down in her favorite cozy chair. Elizabeth and Mary were on the couch beside her, each with her own hot beverage. Tinkerbelle and Pal sat near them and eyed them curiously.

"You're wondering what we're up to, aren't you?" Martha asked the pups.

Mary laughed. "It's been forever since we took an evening to sit together. We've been so busy with the shop and running around trying to find out about the quilt. I'm ready for some sister time."

Elizabeth raised her hand. "Me too," she said. "I know we still have to read the letters from the writing desk, but I think we should just tackle the transcript tonight. Since Betty said the proof is in here, we might not need the letters to tell us who owned the quilt. We can go through them just for ourselves later." She took a breath. "So, whenever you're ready, Martha."

Martha picked up the transcript. "The cover page says they did the recordings in March of 1975." She did the math in her head. "I think that would make Melinda about what? Sixty-eight or so?"

Mary nodded. "Yes, if we're right, and the reason they called themselves the 1907 Girls is because of the year they were born. One of us should remember to ask Betty about that."

Martha turned to the first page and began to read.

"'When I was thirteen years old, my maam said I had to work on my penmanship. Grossmammi said that Maam should make it fun, so Maam gave me a journal. She'd used two pages to record her garden yield but she ripped those pages out. I did the same with my dochders, but I don't know if they will make their children work on their penmanship. Maybe it's not as important anymore as it used to be.

"'We used to have socials for special occasions. I remember one we had, around Grossdaddi's birthday. Grossmammi made ice cream, and even though everyone only had a little, it was delicious. There were cousins there, of course, and friends from the district. Most of us all knew each other, although we didn't get to see each other all that often because we were done with school. There was a girl named Hazel who had just moved into our church district. When some of us were talking, we realized all of us were born in the same year. Hazel told us about a circle where she used to live. The girls wrote letters to each other, and they passed them around. We decided to do that too. I think there were five of us at the time.

"'This was the same year we had a drought. Daed had to sell our cow, and then he had to get a job in town because there were no crops. Maam had another baby coming, and we prayed every day for rain. Of course, we always prayed that Gott's will be done.

"'I remember that the church harvest picnic was canceled that year. Maam said that there just wasn't enough food. And then Maam lost the baby. We were all very sad. Grossdaddi reminded us that we needed *to trust Gott and be joyful, because we welcomed His will, no matter what it was. I tried to think of something I could do that would help us remember to be trusting and joyful and that Gott always cares for us. One of the girls in the circle had suggested that we find something we could make together, so I wrote my circle friends and asked if they would like to make a "joyful quilt" together.*

"'It took a while to hear from everyone, but they all really liked the idea. We decided to each pick three Bible verses about joy or trust or Gott's care to stitch, so we'd have fifteen squares. We all worked very hard over the next year or so, and the result was beautiful.

"'While we worked on our quilt blocks, the drought eventually ended. Daed started working the farm again, Maam got pregnant again—this time with twins—and we had the church harvest dinner again. There was so much food that year! It was as if everyone was making up for the year before. We had tables overflowing with fruit pies, custard pies, all kinds of cakes, cookies, cobblers, and strudels. (Laughter) Now I'm thinking like I'm that thirteen-year-old again, and only mentioning the desserts, aren't I? Well, there were so many tables, filled with all kinds of meats and casseroles and vegetables and breads, we all ate till we couldn't move. We all hoped the hard times were over.'"

Martha lowered the papers to her lap. "That's it. Betty told me she didn't give us the whole thing."

Elizabeth leaned forward and gestured for the papers, and Martha handed them to her. "I wonder if she'd let us read more if we asked?" She skimmed the pages. "I sure would like to hear more about their life back then."

Mary sighed. "It's so sad, to think of the family sitting around the table, with hardly any food on it, and her mom just having lost a baby."

"But they never lost their faith and trust in God," said Elizabeth. "Submission to God's will is one of the Amish core values. Rachel told me they call it *Gelassenheit*. She said they strive to yield to God's will with a content and peaceful spirit."

Martha took a sip of tea, but it had grown cold. She got up and went into the kitchen and stuck her cup in the microwave. She thought about Elizabeth's words as her tea heated. "Gelassenheit," she said out loud. "Gratitude and Gelassenheit."

She carried her tea back into the living room and saw that the dogs had decided it was bedtime and were curled up at Mary's feet.

Mary was holding the transcript pages. She looked up at her sisters. "So do we have our proof now? Melinda says quite plainly that the quilt was her idea."

Elizabeth frowned. "That doesn't mean the quilt was hers. The girls could have made it with the goal of sharing it, like we thought before. The only new thing we learned is that, as you said, it was Melinda's idea."

Mary waved the transcript. "But Betty is sure she just proved the quilt is hers. She's going to be really upset if we don't agree with her."

Martha looked at her watch. Seven thirty. Not too late to pay a visit to Betty.

She set her mug on the coffee table. "Do you think Betty would mind if I pop over for a quick visit?"

"I doubt she'd mind, but do you think you're the best one to go?" Mary looked worried.

Martha looked at her. "Why shouldn't I be the one to go?" she asked.

Mary shrugged. "Well, you're not exactly known for your sensitivity."

Martha rolled her eyes. "We're investigating a mystery. We have to ask questions to get to the truth. Right?" She grinned. "What are you worried about? You know sensitivity is my middle name."

Mary laughed. "Yeah right, and mine is practicality."

Martha gathered her purse and car keys and strode out to her car. As much as she'd hoped they'd find proof, it hadn't happened—yet. She went over her approach to Betty as she covered the short distance to her house. It was sprinkling, and the summer wind had picked up by the time she parked in Betty's driveway. When she knocked on Betty's door. Betty opened it with a smile.

Betty waved her inside. "Oh, Martha, I knew someone would stop by tonight after reading the transcript. I knew I could prove to you that my aenti Melinda was the one who made the quilt." She quickly shut the door behind Martha. "Quite a story she told."

"Yes. It was charming yet hard to read."

"Those were tough times. Did you bring the quilt?"

"Well, actually..."

Betty moved toward the small kitchen. "Set your purse down and stay a while. I'm eager to hear your thoughts about what Aenti Melinda wrote."

"You see, that's why I've come—"

"Would you like pie? I have both apple and custard that I made last night. It's nice to have someone to share them with."

Martha followed Betty into her kitchen and stood by the counter. "We read through the transcript tonight, and it was so interesting. We were wondering if maybe someday we could read the rest of what Melinda remembered about life back then. Your family lived through some really hard times, yet their faith in God remained strong. I'm sure you're proud to have this history, this heritage."

"I always loved my aenti." Betty took two china plates from the cupboard. Then she moved to a drawer and took out two forks. "Did you read the part about the girls meeting and deciding to start a circle?"

"Yes, we did."

Betty paused and fiddled with her kapp string. There was hope in her eyes. "And so you agree with me, that the quilt belonged to Melinda?"

"I was, uh, actually hoping that you could show me where the proof is."

Betty slammed the two forks in her hand onto the counter. "You want me to show you where the proof is? Didn't you read it? Melinda says the quilt was her idea, and that the result was beautiful. It has to be her quilt. Why would another girl keep it if it was Melinda's idea, and it was her family that needed to be reminded to stay joyful?"

"Yes." Martha sighed. "But that's the problem. Melinda said it was her idea, but why would the other girls make the squares if they didn't get to claim partial ownership? She never talked about who it belonged to or what they did with it." She leaned forward, resting her hip against the counter. "Betty, I believe you remember the quilt. I have no doubt Melinda probably had it for a time, but..." She wrinkled her nose, trying to figure out how to say gently what she had to say next. "How do you know the quilt belonged to Melinda? Out of all the girls who were involved in the circle, why would it have gone exclusively to her?"

Betty's head dropped. Her shoulders drooped. She looked at the pie as if it held the answers. "Aenti Melinda talked about the quilt squares and that it was her idea. I-I'd hope that was enough. It seemed enough proof to me."

"Oh, Betty." Martha reached across the counter and put her hand on top of the elderly woman's hand. "I wish it were enough. We're trying. I promise you we are."

Betty lifted her head. She narrowed her gaze and stared intently into Martha's eyes. "I know you are. But is it enough? Will it be enough? Surely there could be more proof..." She pulled her hand out of Martha's grasp and pressed her fingers to her forehead, as if a memory was coming back to her. "Wasn't there a message left on my phone? Something about letters. Did you really find some of the circle letters? I can understand what you're saying about the transcript, but maybe there is something in the letters?" Betty's gaze softened, and Martha really did feel as if she was welcomed to stay for pie.

Martha set her purse down on the table. "Oh yes. We found the letters a couple of days ago inside an old dresser. Then Mary and I found more, far more, today. My sisters and I are going to read through them, and maybe we'll find more actual proof. Or at least that's what I hope."

Betty cut two slices of apple pie, placing them on the plates. "And your sisters? What do they hope?"

"They both want to find the truth. All of us enjoy puzzling out mysteries, so this isn't a hardship for us. We're glad to help."

Betty cocked one eyebrow as she handed over a piece of pie. "And how do they feel about Anne?"

"We know that Anne would be as disappointed to find out the quilt wasn't her cousin's as you would be to find out it wasn't Melinda's. We wish we could find a solution that would make both of you happy."

"Anne already knows that kind of solution doesn't exist," Betty mumbled under her breath.

Martha pulled a chair out from the table and sat down then paused. "What do you mean?"

Betty placed her plate and fork on the table and pulled out her own chair, sitting across from her. Before even taking a bite, she said, "Anne used to be Amish, you know. She didn't think much of making other people happy or of the promises she made to the community when she left the church." Betty looked at her pie and pushed it to the side. Again, her shoulders slumped forward, as if carrying a heavy weight. Her voice trembled as she attempted to hold back tears.

Martha didn't speak, didn't move. The heaviness of Betty's pain hung in the room. There was much more between Anne and Betty than the ownership of a quilt.

"We were schoolmates," Betty said with a quaver in her voice. "Best friends, I would have said. And—and you know how I heard about her leaving? I was at the store, filling my basket, and the shopkeeper told me. 'Sorry to hear about your friend Anne,' he said. 'Out of all the young'uns in our church, I thought she'd be staying.'" Betty sniffled, then grabbed a kitchen towel for her tears. "Only later did Anne come to me and try to explain, but nothing she said made any difference. And now this...How can she break my heart like this again? If Anne saw that quilt any place, it was at my aenti's house. Maybe we even slept under it as girls..."

"I'm sure she doesn't mean to hurt you," Martha said.

"I wish she had just kept to herself," Betty mumbled. "What need does she have for a quilt in her Englisch life?"

Even though Betty asked her these questions, Martha knew they weren't for her. She knew what Betty was really asking. *Did Anne care so little about the friendship we had? And...why? Why does being left out, left behind, hurt so?*

Betty dabbed at her eyes again, and then folded the kitchen towel and set it to the side. "It is just a quilt," she finally mumbled. "I appreciate that you're doing what you can."

It was more than a quilt, Martha knew. The quilt represented Betty's heritage and her most cherished memories, but it also stirred up the sting of a broken friendship.

"I'm just glad we can be of some help." Martha took a bite of her pie and let out a small sound of appreciation. "And oh, Betty! This pie is delicious."

"Yes, it is my aenti's recipe. Aenti Melinda...there was no one like her, really."

"I'm learning that." Martha took another bite. "And even though I'm not thankful for the conflict this is causing between you and Anne, I am thankful for the chance to get to know your aunt and your family better."

"A good family." A fresh brightness filled Betty's face in a way that hadn't been there before. "I'll just pray that He can lead you to the answers you need."

"Me too, Betty." Martha eyed the custard pie, wondering if Betty would offer her a piece of that also. "Me too."

CHAPTER SIXTEEN

Martha opened the front door of the shop, preparing to turn the sign from CLOSED to OPEN, when she noticed a horse and buggy already coming up the lane.

"Someone's up and about early," she called to Mary and Elizabeth. Elizabeth was dusting, and Mary was putting loaves of banana bread into the display case. Martha had been up early baking. She often baked when she needed to think and sort things out in her mind. She'd related her time with Betty to her sisters when she'd arrived home last night.

"This involves so much more than a quilt," she'd told them. "She doesn't understand why Anne would want this quilt, especially since she left the Amish so long ago."

Rachel, Phoebe, and Dorcas entered the shop. Phoebe was carrying a basket covered with a dish towel.

"Oh, look who the wind blew in," Martha called back to her sisters. "Can you fix us all some coffee?"

"You bet." Mary finished her display. "I can make us all some."

Rachel made sure Dorcas wiped her feet on the welcome mat. Strands of Dorcas's dark hair had slipped from her kapp, and Rachel tucked them back inside. "Only make me a cup if you're having some too."

Phoebe held up her basket. "I have your butter and cheese and milk. And me and Dorcas don't like coffee." She looked hopefully at Mary.

Martha chuckled. "I think we can find some milk and cookies for you and Dorcas." She took the basket from Phoebe and hooked elbows with her. "Why don't you and Dorcas go sit in the children's area, and we'll bring you some? There are a couple of new wooden puzzles on the children's shelf you can help Dorcas put together." She nodded at Rachel. "We can take our coffee at the counter."

After depositing the girls at the children's table and getting them settled with their treat, Martha walked to the counter with Mary, who carried a tray with four mugs of coffee.

Rachel looked at Martha with a twinkle in her eye. "I want to kidnap you, if it's all right with your sisters."

"Kidnap me?" Martha looked at her curiously. "Where are we going?"

Rachel looked around to the children's area, checking on the girls, Martha knew. "Well, first I have something I want to run by all three of you."

"We have some new clues about the quilt for you," said Mary.

"The quilt?" Rachel said with a knowing look on her face. "Ja, might it have something to do with Betty Yoder as well? Silas was returning from making a delivery out Betty's way just as we were leaving to come here. He said I might want to check on her later as he didn't see Betty's laundry on the line when he drove by. He worried she might not be feeling well."

Martha nodded. "I suppose an Amish woman not having her laundry out by eight a.m. would be a clear sign there's a problem."

"Out by eight a.m.?" Rachel chuckled. "With someone like Betty, so set in her ways, we're certain there's a problem if the laundry isn't out by six a.m."

Mary put her mug down. Concern was clear on her face. "Should we go check on Betty now?"

"Oh, no. I headed over there straightaway after Silas mentioned his concern. I stopped, just for five minutes, before coming to you. She claims she's under the weather, but before I left she told me about what you found in that transcript of Melinda's, and it set me to thinking..."

"About what?"

"Well, about Betty. About Anne. About the quilt. I dislike conflict. Relationships are so much more important than things, and I have to admit I am struggling not to take sides." She wrapped her hands around the mug and took a sip of her coffee. "As I went along, I started thinking about what you've told me." She took another sip. "I tried to consider how that quilt ended up in an estate sale in the first place, and I remembered something."

"What was that?" Martha looked to Mary and noted hope, mixed with questions, in her sister's gaze.

"Well, back in the early 1980s there was a series of robberies in Amish homes. These robberies occurred while Amish families were in church. We all knew the robbers had to either be ex-Amish or those who were familiar with our ways."

"What does this have to do with the quilt?" Martha asked.

"It is possible that the quilt might have been stolen then. So, it could have been with Anne's family or with Betty's family and—"

"And someone stole it? Which is why it turned up in an estate sale?"

Mary grabbed Martha's arm. "That's a possibility. It could explain why the person who sold the estate to Angelina didn't want his or her information getting out."

Elizabeth nodded. "And didn't you say that there were a lot of personal items? Those are usually things that family members want to keep."

"But if they were stolen," Rachel chimed in, "the thief would not care about those things. And that is why I want to take you on a field trip. I remember hearing about the robberies back then, and I thought we should head to the library."

"The library?"

"We can look up old newspapers from the time."

Martha lifted an eyebrow. "Can't we just google them?"

Rachel laughed. "Remember where we are. I suspect there is no funding to put old newspapers online."

"That makes sense." Martha looked at her sisters.

Elizabeth lifted both hands in the air. "Don't worry. We can manage here."

"We'll be back before too long," Martha assured her.

Mary turned to Rachel. "How would Phoebe and Dorcas feel about staying here while you two are doing your sleuthing? There's plenty to keep them busy, and I'll keep an eye on them."

Rachel hugged her. "That would be wonderful, and I'm sure they'll be thrilled. They've been after me to bring them to look at your new children's books."

"I'll get my purse and car keys," Martha said, gathering the mugs onto the tray.

"I was thinking we should take the buggy. It is not good to leave my horse standing so long."

"But it will take twice as long."

"Twice as long to drive there, yes, but also twice as long to enjoy each other's company." Rachel looked at Mary. "Unless that would keep you away too long?"

Mary grinned and waved at them. "Martha always comes back sweeter when she's been with you, Rachel," she teased. "Keep her as long as you like."

Martha laughed. "Well, if you put it that way. Let me go get my purse."

Ten minutes later Martha was sitting next to Rachel in the front seat of the buggy, and the horse was trotting down the road. "Do you really think the quilt could have been stolen from the rightful owner?" she asked Rachel.

"It is worth looking into, right?"

Martha nodded and settled back for the drive. It took them twenty minutes to get to the library, and as the minutes passed Martha found herself enjoying the ride, and not only for the pleasant conversation she shared with Rachel. The *clip-clop* of the horse's hooves on the pavement put her at ease. She enjoyed studying the farms as they drove by. She appreciated the summer colors and the bushes adorned in flowers—things she usually sped by when she was driving.

When they reached the library, the librarian was all too eager to help them find what they needed on the microfiche. Martha and Rachel settled in, side by side, as she showed them how to use the machine.

"Thank you so much, Miss Fraser," Martha said.

"Oh please, call me Fanny." The young woman wore two long braids and looked about sixteen, but Martha guessed she was older than that. Martha knew she was getting old when everyone around town, from the library to the doctor's office, looked as if they should still be in high school.

"I've made a note of what you're looking for, and I'll check some other sources too," Fanny said. "A lot of records are in the public domain now. I'm not sure if I'll find anything, but I'll be happy to look."

Rachel stared up at Fanny, wide-eyed. "And just think, I thought the library was only for checking out books." She turned to Martha. "It was Hannah who told me about the microfiche. Her teacher brought her class here last year when they were writing local history reports."

"I remember when that Amish school group came in," Fanny commented. "I was surprised because I thought the Amish weren't allowed to use technology."

"Oh, we can use it as it is needed, just not in our homes," Rachel explained. "In our homes we try to stay as self-sufficient as possible." She smiled. "I have given it much thought as my children are growing, and I am glad that Silas and I are, after God, of course, the most important influence in their lives."

Fanny smiled back at her. "I think that's wonderful." She turned to go back to her desk. "I'll do what I can to help you track down any information on those robberies."

"If it'll take too much time..." Martha's voice trailed off.

Fanny tossed one of her braids over her shoulder. "That's what I'm here for. And I wasn't even alive in the eighties, so it'll be interesting to see what life was like back then too."

Martha and Rachel offered each other knowing looks, and then Martha said, "Thank you, I appreciate that. It was an interesting time to be alive."

It didn't take long to scan the headlines of the weekly newspaper, and they soon found the headline they were looking for, in November 1982.

"'String of Amish Home Burglaries Shakes Community,'" Martha read aloud.

Together, she and Rachel read the articles, and they discovered that Rachel was right. Over a dozen Amish homes were robbed while families were in church, all within a few weeks' time. Numerous items were stolen, especially Amish handicrafts and quilts. The only problem was, the newspaper did not mention which families the items had come from.

Leaning back in her chair, Martha rubbed her eyes, suddenly realizing how weary they were from reading the small print on the microfiche slides. "Well, all I have to say is that our quilt being one of the stolen ones is possible, but there's really no way of knowing it was for sure. This quilt could have been one taken from the rightful owner, but we still don't have proof of who the rightful owner was."

Rachel turned off the microfiche machine and stood. "And if we ask Anne and Betty about the robberies—even if their families were among those who were robbed—we still will not have proof that this quilt was one of the ones stolen." Rachel crossed her arms over her chest. "I am sorry, Martha, I am afraid this was a wild-goose chase."

"Not really. A least it gives us another possibility." Martha also stood. "It's good to have more avenues to consider. I just wish there was something that could definitively point us to the rightful owner, and we could put this conflict between Anne and Betty to rest."

Rachel chuckled. "And I think it would feel good to solve another mystery, right? You and your sisters are enjoying the challenge, I think, ja?"

Martha picked up her purse, preparing for the buggy ride home. "Yes, you're right about that too." They said goodbye to Fanny and left the library. As Martha climbed into the buggy, she said, "I haven't given up hope that the letters will give us some more clues."

Rachel gave her a questioning look as she unhitched the horse. "What letters?"

It took most of their thirty-minute ride for Martha to tell Rachel about the letters they'd found, and as they were nearing Secondhand Blessings, Martha had made up her mind they needed to go through the rest of the letters from the writing desk as soon as possible.

"You know, Martha," Rachel said, throwing a quick glance Martha's way while she flicked the reins to urge the horse onward, "all this talk of quilt circles and such makes me realize that

I should be holding a quilting circle again. The last circle I was a part of finished a project for a benefit auction recently, and we all decided to take a break during the busy season of spring planting. We most definitely need to get started again. What would you think about the idea of us holding our regular circle times at Secondhand Blessings? That way, the tourists who stop in to shop could see what all is involved in the actual making of an Amish quilt. And it would be a most convenient place for our ladies to gather."

"Oh, Rachel," Martha exclaimed, "I believe that's a wonderful idea! We have that nice open space near the front register that would be a perfect place for you to gather. Let me run it by Mary and Elizabeth to be sure, but I'm positive they will agree!"

Rachel nodded. "*Wunderbar*! Just let me know if they say yes, and I will contact the women I believe might be interested."

As they turned down the lane to the Classen property, Martha sat straighter when she noticed a large delivery truck parked in the driveway.

"Are you expecting a delivery?" Rachel asked.

"Yes. Or it could be that Mary has a visitor."

"Mary, really?" Rachel flipped the reins as she turned the buggy onto the lane. "I think that is wonderful. Mary is still quite young."

"That she is."

"And who knows," Rachel said as she pulled up to the shop and stopped the horses. "Maybe this whole episode has not been about the quilt at all."

"I've had the same feeling," Martha said, preparing to disembark from the buggy. She looked at the delivery truck again.

She'd meant to ask Angelina for more information about Samuel. "Thank you for your idea and your help, Rachel. It really is appreciated."

Rachel waved a hand in the air. "I am not sure if it was any help, but it was nice to spend some time with you. Should I dare hope the girls are ready to go by now?"

Martha smiled. "And do I dare hope that Mary or Elizabeth has found a piece of the puzzle that will help solve this mystery?"

CHAPTER SEVENTEEN

The first thing Elizabeth noticed when she entered the back room of Secondhand Blessings was Mary chatting with Samuel, who stood by an old bookcase. Was that the delivery, that old bookcase? Is that what Mary had been excited about having refinished? If it was, Elizabeth wasn't sure it was worth the time. The bookcase looked as if it was nearly falling apart, and it had been painted too many times. It would take hours to peel all the paint off and do anything with whatever wood was left behind. Yet the way Mary looked at the piece you'd think the driver was delivering a priceless piece of art.

"Elizabeth, come on over. Samuel delivered the bookcase for us without charge. Isn't that nice?"

"Hello, Samuel. Thank you for making the delivery." Elizabeth eyed the bookcase again, attempting not to show her displeasure with it.

"You're welcome. It's nice to meet another one of Mary's sisters."

"It's nice to meet you too, and I'm thankful for the help you gave my sisters yesterday. I know they enjoyed reading the letters they found."

"And have you found any solid connection with the quilt?" he asked, turning back to Mary. "Angelina explained the situation to me."

Mary shook her head. "Not yet. We haven't read them all though. Still, we're enjoying learning more about Melinda Yoder and the other girls."

Elizabeth ran her hands down her red-checkered apron that read *Secondhand Blessings* on the bodice. "We found out that the girls made the quilt when the Yoder family hit hard times."

Samuel cleared his throat. "Melinda Yoder...yes, I know exactly who you are talking about. Her family's property isn't far from ours. It's a beautiful, thriving farm." He tipped the bookcase off his dolly and prepared to go. "Let me know if I can do anything else for you all."

Mary placed a hand on his arm. "Let me walk you out, and I'll get you some of Martha's baked goods to take home. Thank you so much for the delivery."

Elizabeth followed them into the shop and went to the children's area to check on the girls. They were in the middle of a puppet show that, from what she could tell, was chiefly about the animals on their farm.

Martha and Rachel came in just then, and Rachel gathered her girls to hurry home. Martha spent the next few minutes sharing about what they'd discovered at the library. "Rachel's memories were correct. There were a number of thefts in the early 1980s, and family heirlooms were stolen. But there were no names in the articles, so we have no way of knowing if it's even possible if the girls' quilt was one of them."

"And even if Melinda did own the quilt at one time, she could have sold it." Mary's brow furrowed. "Or maybe she didn't sell it, and it wasn't stolen, and she gave it as a gift..." She rubbed her forehead, as if that would help her make sense of every-thing. "Is anyone else getting confused?"

Elizabeth pursed her lips. "I don't know if Melinda would have sold the quilt. It seems like she would have offered it to one of the other girls before she would do that. The idea of it being stolen or given away seems much more possible."

"What if her family fell on hard times again, and they had to sell whatever they could to survive?" Mary wasn't giving up.

Elizabeth considered this idea. "I suppose that could hap-pen, but I still think it would be one of the last possessions Melinda would part with."

Martha rubbed her hands together. "We have to face that we may never have the answer—" Her words were interrupted by the door opening and a group of women hustling in.

"Oh, look at this place. It's as wonderful as the librarian told us." A young woman with bright red hair hurried inside. She looked just like a grown-up Anne of Green Gables. "I think we might be able to discover our own piece of history here."

Martha approached the women, her smile wide. "Was it Fanny who told you about us?"

The woman turned to her friend. "Was that the librarian's name?"

"Yes. I love that name." The tall blonde wore overalls and had a baby on her hip. Her hair was tied up in a bandana, and she wore a peasant blouse and capris. She pinched her baby's cheek. "Almost as cute as the name Polly."

The baby cooed and grinned, clapping her hands together.

Everything old is new again, I suppose, Elizabeth thought. "How can I help you, ladies?"

"We're looking for vintage clothes and old records." The red-haired woman's eyes brightened. "Is that a record player I see over there?" She pointed to a table with old electronics.

Mary stepped forward. "Yes, and it works. We tried it ourselves." She swayed from side to side and waved her finger in the air as if doing the bop.

"Wonderful," the blonde squealed. "But first we also came to deliver a message." She turned to Martha.

"A message?"

"Yes, the librarian heard us talking about coming here and asked us to tell you she found more information you'll want to see. She's off for the rest of the day, but she's supposed to be back tomorrow."

Martha smiled. "Thank you for telling us. It was kind of Fanny to send a messenger."

Elizabeth waved the women forward. "Now, let me show you that record player. I know the perfect record to play on it too. You ladies ever heard of Elvis?"

CHAPTER EIGHTEEN

T he sweet scent of fresh-from-the-oven chocolate chip cookies came with Martha into the library on Wednesday morning. It carried over the shelves of books and caused a group of small heads to turn her direction. Preschool story time was in full swing, and with the scent of a yummy treat, the toddlers soon forgot about the story being read to them, and a few wandered in her direction. Martha hurried to the counter and handed Fanny the bag of cookies.

"I'm so sorry. I didn't realize my gift would draw a crowd."

Fanny tucked the bag under the counter. "Then this is your first Toddler Time. We like to think it's about the books, but it's really about the snacks."

One of the toddlers approached Martha, and then seeing that she no longer held the bag of treats, he attempted to get behind the counter until his mother swooped him up. "That's not for you, Liam. One more story, and we'll get out your bran puffs, I promise."

Martha watched as the mother scooted little Liam back to story time, then she looked to Fanny with a lifted eyebrow. "Bran puffs?"

Fanny nodded with all seriousness. "Organic." She pretended to shudder. "I'd rather have what smells so delicious in the bag, but you didn't have to do that, really."

Martha adjusted her purse on her shoulder and leaned closer as the singing of "The Wheels on the Bus" rang out from the story-time rug. "I'm thankful for your help."

Fanny opened her mouth and answered her, but her words were lost in the singing. With a shake of her head, she motioned Martha to follow her into a back room. An older woman with tight gray curls was sitting at a desk taping a dust jacket on a book.

"Karen, would you mind watching the front? I have some printouts here that I want to show Martha—"

"Martha from Secondhand Blessings?" Karen asked, springing to her feet. "Oh, I was wanting to meet you. Fanny here told me about how you're going out of your way to find the rightful owner of a quilt. I've never known a business owner to be so caring and diligent. We've been telling all our patrons."

The excitement in the woman's face caught Martha by surprise. Karen acted as if Martha was a celebrity or something.

"It's not a hardship," Martha assured her. "My sisters and I enjoy a good mystery."

Fanny waved at Karen, who hurried out of the room to help a patron. "Yes, well, maybe your sisters will find this helpful."

She motioned for Martha to sit, then she sat in the chair beside her. "I've found a couple of articles that might help you understand the robberies better. There was even an academic study done on what could have started the rash. It wasn't just a *rumspringa* gone bad, as some thought at the time. Instead, it looks like a group of hooligans were targeting the homes at a vulnerable time—just like some thieves target homes of the grieving during funerals."

"Yes, that's what Rachel said." Martha nodded. "Whoever committed the thefts struck at a time when they knew no one would be home."

"Exactly." Fanny placed a printout in front of Martha. It was filled with photographs of quilts. "They never caught who was responsible, but they did retrieve some of the quilts. It seems the thief had posted a box to be shipped, but it hadn't been taped up well enough. When the shipping clerk attempted to tape the box back up he noticed a quilt. He'd been following the burglaries in the paper, so he called the police."

"Amazing that the shipping clerk was paying attention. Kudos to him. Did the families get their quilts back?"

"Yes, eventually. They were held in evidence for a while."

"Why would someone mail them?"

"Look at this." Fanny placed another printout in front of her. "I'm sure you realize that many people consider Amish quilts to be works of art. There's quite a market for them, especially older ones." Fanny paused, narrowed her gaze, and leaned toward Martha, lowering her voice. "In fact, part of me wonders if that's what the fight is about. Surely the quilt can't belong to both women. Maybe one of them wants it so badly because she knows she can sell it for a lot of money."

"Oh, I'm sure that's not true!" Martha exclaimed. The surprised look on Fanny's face made it clear that Martha had been a bit too indignant in her reaction.

"You would know better than I, seeing as how you are acquainted with them, but one never knows these days. People can sure surprise you." Fanny picked up the papers and straightened them. She placed them on the table before Martha. "I'm afraid I've become too suspicious."

"I certainly understand, given all we see and hear in the news." Martha picked up the top paper to take a closer look. "Still, I know them very well. Anne was my mother's good friend. I know her character. She wouldn't lie. And Betty is an Amish woman…"

Fanny flipped her braid. "Of course, *most* of the Amish in this community are very trustworthy."

Martha noticed Fanny put emphasis on *most*. She supposed humans were humans no matter their walk of life.

Fanny showed her a book. "I found this about the art of Amish quilts. Feel free to check it out. But basically the book talks about how the Amish never consider their quilts to be art. After all, they're usually made out of leftover scraps of material…"

"And they would never consider a quilt just something to look at."

"Exactly." Fanny smiled, but it wasn't as friendly a smile as before Martha's overreaction. Thankfully, her sisters knew that she often spoke before she thought things through, and they didn't take it to heart. Chuck had always been patient with her too—*thank You, Lord, for that*—but she was starting to see that she needed to work harder on her reactions at times, especially since she represented Secondhand Blessings now. Maybe being more patient with people and situations was part of Gelassenheit.

Fanny flipped through the book's pages, pausing on a photograph of an Amish sampler quilt that created a vibrant pattern of triangles and squares on a background of black. "I know the woman who made this would consider it vain to display her quilt..." She ran her fingers over the page. "But it's so beautiful, I would display it in my home instead of a painting. It's hard to believe the Amish make quilts like this for common use."

Martha read through the list of stolen items again. "Quilts, rocking horses, furniture, linens..." She paused on that one.

"My guess would be from young women's hope chests," Fanny said. "They stitch the most beautiful linens in preparation for marriage someday."

Martha shook her head. "What kind of person would steal from a hope chest? But I think you're right, Fanny. Whoever committed the thefts knew what they were doing. It appears they stole items that seemed ordinary to the Amish but would be desirable to collectors."

Yet, even as Martha found this interesting, it still didn't help with their quilt. The fact was, two women, neither of whom were interested in making money on the sale of such a treasure, were still waiting to hear what Martha and her sisters discovered.

CHAPTER NINETEEN

Martha made it back to the shop in time to take over so Elizabeth and Mary could have lunch, then the afternoon passed quickly as she and Elizabeth waited on customers and updated displays. In the back room, Mary sorted through boxes of seasonal decorations that had come in that morning. She was singing along to praise songs playing over the radio. By closing time, she had added several Fourth of July displays, featuring fireworks and all things red, white, and blue.

As they walked to the house after locking up the shop, Martha spoke up from behind the other two. "Do you have time to go through letters tonight? I thought we could sort them by date and tackle them that way."

Mary turned and walked backward as she answered. "I'm going to meet Samuel at the café for a sandwich, but I'll be back by eight or so. He has a late delivery to make for Angelina tonight. Can you wait for—oops!" Her heel caught on a raised stone on the walkway, and she would have fallen if Elizabeth hadn't caught her arm.

"If you're not careful the only waiting we'll be doing is in the ER," she scolded her little sister. "You need to be more careful, Mary. You're not a teenager anymore."

Mary sighed. "I know. But I have a hard time remembering that."

Martha caught up to them. "We'll wait for you, Mary. You go and have a good time."

When they got in the house, Mary went upstairs to get ready to go, and by the time Martha had her casserole out of the fridge and in the oven, Mary was out the door.

Elizabeth stuck her head in the kitchen. "I'm going to get the animals fed."

"That sounds good to me," said Martha. "I think I'll give Trish a call. I haven't talked to her in a couple of weeks."

She punched Trish's speed dial number on her phone, put her phone on Speaker, and laid it on the counter. While it rang, she got lettuce and tomatoes out of the fridge. By the time she'd collected the cutting board and knife, Trish answered.

"Hey, Mom! What's up?"

"Nothing too earth-shaking. How about with you? How's Jared? How are the kids?"

"They're crazy, as usual. We just had the end-of-the-year school parties. You remember what happened last year, when Celeste announced in the middle of preschool graduation that preschool was way too boring, and she was so smart she was going to skip kindergarten and join Elliott in first grade?"

Martha laughed. "I remember. You were mortified. Jared was mortified. Elliott was mortified. He did not want his sister anywhere near him. Celeste's teacher and I were laughing too hard to be mortified."

Trish sighed. "Yeah, well, this year she told us she has no intention of going to first grade this fall. Her best friend, Jordan—he lives next door—is a year behind her, and she's decided that repeating kindergarten is a small price to pay to be with him."

Martha laughed again. "That's my girl."

There was a pause. Then Trish asked, "So, Mom, how are you? I was thinking, maybe you'd like to come here for a few days? Seeing as next week..."

Martha got a bowl out of the cupboard for a salad. "Oh, honey, I really appreciate that. But I think if you call me that day—and get Craig and Kyle to call too—I'll be okay. Unless you need me to come, I'll stay busy here."

"Of course I'll call you. And I'm sure the boys will too. Now, what else is happening?"

Martha finished getting the salad ready while she told Trish about the quilt mystery.

"That's so cool, Mom. I wish my friends and I had thought about doing something like that when we were their age. I'll try to remember it when Celeste's a teenager. Unfortunately, she'll probably be acting like one by the time she's eight, and instead of a quilt, she'll want her friends to make a time machine."

Martha was about to answer when she heard a crash in the background. "What was that?"

"I don't know—gotta go, love you, Mom!"

Martha chuckled as she hit the END button on her screen. Never a dull moment with her grandchildren. And that was only two of them. Craig's two and Kyle's little one were equally smart, equally delightful, and equally adored by Grandma.

Mary returned a little before eight, and the three sisters gathered with mugs of decaf tea in the living room. Martha divided the letters into three stacks and gave a stack to each of her sisters. "I've written down the names of the girls who wrote the letters we already have....Let's just take turns reading and see what we can find out."

"That's as good a way to do it as any, I suppose," said Elizabeth. "I can start." She read from the first letter on her stack. "This one is dated April 2, 1922, and it's from Katie Filbrun. Remember? She's the one who chose to stitch Proverbs 3:5. *"My daed has been fit to be tied, because one of our cows has learned to open the gate on her stall and she keeps getting out. My daed had my bruders watch her for a whole day so they could see how she was getting out. And how do you think she does it? With her tongue! She loops her tongue around the handle and pulls it out of the slot, and she has even learned that there are two of them, and she can do both."* Elizabeth stopped reading and turned the page over. Martha could see that she was skimming the paper. "The rest is about the new kittens and how many eggs they gathered in the week."

Martha laughed. "What a smart cow—I would love to see that." She picked up the letter on the top of her pile. "Okay, this one is dated October 20, 1921, and is from Hazel. *"You girls would not believe how many pies Maam, Sarah, Lucille, and I made yesterday for today's social. I rolled out dough for twenty-six pies! I don't think we've ever had such a crop of apples, and, of course, we had to make many pumpkin pies. The house smelled so good! We had a time keeping the little ones' fingers out of the filling."* Martha read ahead quickly then said, "She goes on about the social and what she ate and the games they played. Nothing about any quilt or project they were doing."

"This one is from Irma, Anne's cousin." Mary began reading from the letter in her hand. *"Sometimes it is so hard to be the*

baby of the family. Everyone else is either going through their rumsp-
ringa or courting or married. I am the only one who has to stay home
at night. I wish you girls lived close to me so we could be everyday
friends.'" Mary sighed. "Boy, do I remember feeling like that.
You two were dating and going out, and I had to stay behind at
home. I even had to go to bed before you came home. I guess
even little Amish girls want to grow up faster."

Elizabeth laughed. "You've gotten your revenge, baby sis.
Here you are, going out with more men than we can keep track
of, while we old ladies sit at home."

"Speaking of," Martha said. "You never did say anything
about how your date with Samuel went. Are we going to see
him at our dinner table anytime soon?"

Mary shook her head. "I don't think so. He's a nice guy,
but, I don't know, things were pretty awkward between us for
some reason. I just felt like he was trying too hard to impress
me, and that made me nervous." She smiled sweetly at her
sisters. "So, if either of you are interested, I'll gladly pass him
along to you."

Elizabeth and Martha both gave her a raspberry, but
Martha was secretly glad that Samuel and Mary hadn't hit it
off. She was rooting for Bill Richmond. He and Mary had been
friends for many years before Mary married Brian and left
Bird-in-Hand. Martha was a big fan of marrying a good friend.
Another thing to be grateful for, Lord. I truly did marry my very best
friend.

The sisters spent another hour or so reading the letters,
and although they were delightful, and some of the girls
mentioned the squares they were stitching, they didn't learn

anything more about the quilt's ownership. Martha laid down the last one and sighed heavily. "Well, that's it. Not any more to go on than we had before."

Mary gathered her letters and straightened the stack. "Yes, but don't you feel like you almost know these girls? I almost feel like part of their circle."

Martha yawned and stood, handing her stack of letters to Mary. "I do too. Oh, and that reminds me! Rachel would like to hold a quilting circle at our shop. I thought it sounded like a wonderful idea, but I told her I'd run the idea past you two first. I think our customers would be fascinated to witness how a quilt is made, don't you?" She looked from Mary to Elizabeth and back again. Both sisters were nodding in agreement.

"What a great idea!" Mary laughed. "I'm just sorry I didn't come up with it first."

"Okay, then. I'll let Rachel know she's welcome to start any time." Martha sighed in contentment, then she grinned and exchanged a meaningful glance with Elizabeth. "Now, off to bed for all of us. But, Mary, I want you to know, we really appreciate your thoughtfulness about Samuel. We hope you have sweet dreams tonight. Whatever you do, try not to think about cows' tongues right before you go to sleep."

"Or pumpkin pies by the dozens," Elizabeth added.

Mary groaned. "You two are so mean to me sometimes. Now that's all I'll think of."

Martha smiled. Mission accomplished.

CHAPTER TWENTY

The familiar strident voice of Reddy the rooster roused Martha from her sleep. She'd been dreaming about the quilt for the second night in a row. This time she pictured the girls in their Amish dresses and kapps sitting around a quilting frame. Which was better than the night before, when she'd dreamed of quilts dancing around her and then wrapping around her feet so she couldn't walk. She'd awakened to find Butterscotch, their orange tabby cat, lying on her feet.

Martha remembered going to an Amish sewing circle with her mother once when she was about twelve. She'd broken her wrist a few days prior, when she fell off their tire swing, and had stayed home from school. She'd expected to be curled up on the couch with a book all day, but instead her mother took her down the road to a neighbor's house. Mama had always enjoyed handiwork, and when the Amish ladies had seen her skill, they'd invited her to join them.

Martha rose and dressed as the pleasant memory continued to unfold in her thoughts. She hadn't thought of that special day with her mother in twenty years at least, and it surprised her how much was coming back to her. There had been older teen girls caring for the little ones and making lunch in the kitchen. There had been conversation and laughter around the circle. Even a few tears had been shed as women shared theirs joys and burdens.

She'd been propped up on the couch, and Mama had sat at the sewing frame. She'd stayed quiet, seemingly listening to the other women.

They'd eaten lunch sitting around the long wooden table with benches on either side. Mama had to help her with her sandwich and sweet pickles, since she had a hard time eating with her left hand. Then, after lunch, they'd returned home. Martha had wanted to stay and watch the women continue to sew, but Mother had said Martha needed to rest. She still remembered all eyes on them as they'd left and the way her mother had smiled and waved.

She was still thinking of that day and how much she missed her mother when she went down to the kitchen. She whipped up a double batch of strawberry muffins and got them in the oven. Then she made coffee and put some bread in the toaster.

The shuffling of footsteps joined by the sound of two dogs walking into the kitchen met her ears. Martha turned to see Elizabeth standing in the doorway. Elizabeth smiled as she entered the kitchen. "You're making coffee, thank heavens. Mary's going to need it. She told me every time she closed her eyes last night she saw cows eating pumpkin pies with long, long tongues."

Martha laughed. "The poor thing. She deserved every bit of it. Yes, the coffee is almost ready, and I've made a couple of pieces of toast to help me get going on a real breakfast." She pointed to the toaster. "Want one?"

Tinkerbelle and Pal headed straight for the back door. Elizabeth said, "Yes, please," and went to let them out. When she returned, she pulled a mug from the cabinet. She set the mug on the counter and tightened the belt around her waist before pouring her coffee.

When the toast popped up, Martha put it on a plate and handed it to Elizabeth. She took her own plate and mug, and she and Elizabeth sat at the table sharing a butter knife and passing honey and homemade jam to each other. While they ate, Martha told Elizabeth about her memory of the sewing circle. But instead of smiling, her sister's brow furrowed.

"Oh, I remember that. It was a sad time."

Martha lifted her hand and twisted her wrist. "Oh, it did hurt, but you'd never know it was broken."

"I'm not talking about that. Don't you remember why those ladies had an open spot in their sewing circle?"

Martha searched her mind, trying to remember more about how her mom ended up at the sewing circle, but all she could remember was her own broken wrist and the interesting time she had at the Amish woman's house.

"Do you remember the day after the sewing circle? That was the first day Anne ever came to our house."

"I remember." Martha placed her coffee cup on the table. "Mama knew her from the fruit and vegetable stand that Anne used to run."

"Mama knew Anne's family too, but she wasn't as close to them as she was to Anne." Elizabeth added cream to her coffee. "Mama really got to know Anne after she found out at the sewing circle that her family had shunned her for leaving the church. She knew that when they did, Anne couldn't go to any Amish houses anymore."

"Are you saying that Mama was filling in Anne's spot at the sewing circle?"

"Yes, but she didn't know it until she got there. And when she found out, she felt horrible."

Martha rubbed her brow. "But how do you remember this? How do you know?"

"It was a few days later. I'd gotten angry about something Mama wouldn't let me do. I said something about maybe I'd run away and find a better family"—she held up her hand at Martha's open mouth—"I know, I know, but in my defense, I was fourteen. Mama and I laughed about it many years later. Anyway, she told me about Anne having to leave her family, and how she couldn't even join them for fun times anymore. Mama felt so bad. She said it was really uncomfortable for her, being at that sewing circle."

"But I don't remember that. I don't remember anyone being upset. They acted as if everything was normal."

"Yes, and that's what bothered her the most. If someone dies then everyone talks about them. They mourn them. They miss them. But when you shun someone it isn't like that. It's not as if they're dead. It's almost as if they were never alive."

"Oh, that is horrible." Martha gripped her mug. "Betty Yoder—she was there. I do remember that."

"And it was after that when Mama reached out to Anne. She figured that with so many of her friends no longer speaking to her, she would need a friend."

"You're right, that is sad." Martha finished her toast. "Have you seen Anne lately?"

"Not since the day she was in the shop and talked to you about the quilt. How about you?"

"I haven't talked to her since Saturday, when I called and told her about the letters. Would it be all right with you if I called her and asked her to meet me for coffee sometime today?"

Elizabeth rose from her chair. "I think that's a good idea. Thinking about all of this makes me think about this quilt differently. I mean, the Amish ladies already have so much of their heritage. I'm sure Anne left so much behind when she and Aaron left the community. Maybe she should be the one to get the quilt after all."

Martha stood and put their dishes in the sink just as Mary walked into the kitchen, holding Butterscotch and yawning. "Hey there, sleepyhead," Martha said. "Would you like some pumpkin muffins for breakfast?"

"Lucky for you I'm holding this cat and can't throw something at you," grumbled Mary. She looked at Elizabeth. "What's this about you thinking Anne should have the quilt?"

Elizabeth looked from Mary to Martha and back again. "Oh, no. You two aren't going to get me to referee this early in the morning." She pointed to the window. "Look at that gorgeous sun. Let's get a quick breakfast and get out to the shop."

While Elizabeth cut up a couple of oranges and Mary made more toast, Martha got busy heating water for oatmeal.

The more she thought about it, the more she realized that the one person they needed to talk to was the one who'd been the most silent. Anne Hostetler had been the first one to recognize the quilt and express interest in it. Yet she'd also been quiet since Betty had claimed it was hers. Yes, it was time to hear from Anne.

CHAPTER TWENTY-ONE

Anne entered the front door of Mel's Coffee Café and waved. Martha put her mug down and stood as Anne approached and gave her a quick embrace. "I'm so glad you've come. I feel bad for not reaching out to you sooner."

Anne smiled as she slid into a chair. She was tall and thin, and she still dressed conservatively, even though she'd left the Amish years ago. Her cheeks were naturally flushed, and her hazel eyes looked more gray today. Her gaze was warm, yet from the way she nibbled at her lower lip, she seemed nervous.

"I'm just glad to see you today. Aaron left to visit his brother in Ohio day before yesterday, and my company is gone, so the house is much too quiet." She tilted her head. "Has anyone ever told you how much you look like your mother? It almost took my breath away, seeing you sitting there. I thought it was her for a moment, although her hair was gray the last years I knew her."

Martha nodded and smiled. "Yes, I've been told that a time or two since I moved back here. I never tire of hearing it."

Anne picked up the spoon from her place setting and put it back down. "From what you said when you called, I guess you want to talk about the quilt."

"Yes. We've noticed we haven't heard much from you after Betty decided to claim the quilt too."

Anne lifted her empty cup to the server walking by, signaling that she'd like some coffee when the waitress was able. Then she turned her attention back to Martha. "I lived too many years feeling as if I was someone who brought trouble to the Amish community." She sighed. "I want the quilt. I really do, but I also don't want to make any more trouble."

"There was trouble between you and Betty when you left, wasn't there? She still feels betrayed after all these years. She's upset that she didn't find out about your leaving the church from you."

Anne looked down at the table. "There are things I would have done differently if I had them to do over again," she said. "Not the leaving part. Aaron and I never regretted that. But the way it happened...it's hard for me to blame Betty for how she feels. In the end, it was easier not to tell her myself."

The waitress came and filled their cups, and Martha began to tell Anne about all she and her sisters had been doing to research the quilt. It took two cups of coffee for each of them for Martha to explain about the people they'd talked to and about the letters they'd found.

Anne perked up at the mention of those. "Oh, they sound wonderful. I'd love to read them. I bet the Lancaster Mennonite Historical Society would find them interesting too."

"Yes, there's a lot of history in the letters, but maybe we should let the families decide whether they want them to go public. That is, if we can find the families. We don't have any addresses, and if the girls got married, as is probably the case, we wouldn't know their married names."

"That makes sense," Anne said. "Some of the families probably wouldn't want an ancestor's letter put on display."

Martha tucked a strand of hair behind her ear. "Is it hard, Anne? Me asking about the quilt and digging up the past?"

Anne smiled ruefully. "Who says you're digging up the past? To do that it would have actually had to have been buried for a while." She shrugged. "Aaron and I knew what we were doing when we left the church. Shunning has eased up some in modern days, but we knew what we were leaving behind. My family felt as if I'd abandoned them. They also acted as if it was all Aaron's fault. The thing is, I'd thought about leaving even before I met him." The softest smile touched Anne's lips, and her gaze moved to the wall over Martha's shoulder, as if the older women saw something there—as if a memory played upon the cream-colored plaster.

"My grandmother gave me her Bible, you see." Anne's voice was low. "I used to read it to her before bed. That was my task. I'd go to the *dawdy haus* and read by candlelight. On my twelfth birthday, Grandmother told me that the Bible was mine. She told me to keep reading. She said that I didn't need to know what the bishop thought as much as I needed to know what God thought." Emotions caused Anne's words to catch in her throat, and even though the older woman looked her seventy-odd years, Martha could almost spot the twelve-year-old girl in her eyes.

Martha didn't know what to say. And truthfully she didn't know if she should say anything at all. Instead, she simply reached out and took Anne's hand in hers.

"There were times"—Anne's voice was hardly any more than a whisper—"that I almost wished I had listened to the bishop more than God. But when I kept reading, I realized that there was nowhere in the Bible that says we have to live Plain in order to make it to heaven. Yet Aaron and I found out there were times that living by grace was harder than living by the law. Sometimes it's just easier to follow the rules, if you know what I mean."

Martha nodded, feeling the woman's words go deep. "I do. I find it's easier to live by a to-do list sometimes."

"But life isn't about getting things done, now is it? Aaron used to remind me of that when I tried to fill the hole my family had left with activity. He made me get out and meet people." Anne reached over and patted Martha's hand. "He has always said there is much more to life than staying busy. Relationships and people. If those didn't matter, neither of us would be sitting here." The waitress stopped by to top off their coffees, and Anne took another sip. "And if there wasn't a problem with the quilt, you and I would have missed out on this time together."

"And I wouldn't have learned so much about you...about your experiences." Martha smiled. "I always knew you as Mama's friend who used to be Amish. I never really thought about what leaving meant for you."

"Part of me still feels Amish inside." Anne pressed one finger to her cheek. "I have so many good memories."

"Can you tell me your memories about the quilt?" Martha asked.

"Oh yes." Anne straightened in her seat. "I remember it being in my sister's house. I told you, our cousin Irma made it."

Martha nodded. It was a name she'd read in the letters.

"Well, let me backtrack. My sister used it as a bedspread even before she was married. Mother told Grace to save it for her hope chest, but she wouldn't think of it. She insisted that something so thoughtfully made needed to be used."

"And then what happened to the quilt?"

"The quilt went with Grace when she was married. Her husband Harvey had built a large room for their future children when he built their house. That was a guest room before the first baby came, and that's where I used to stay. That's why I remember the quilt. Sometimes, when I couldn't sleep, I'd lie there and read the scripture verses by moonlight."

Anne sighed and rubbed her hand over her heart as if the memory pained her. "That was more than sixty years ago, but that quilt brings back such fond memories. The verses on the quilt helped me after—" She paused. "After Aaron and I left. When I got especially lonely for my family, I remembered the joy promised in those quilt verses, and they gave me strength. Isn't that how God's Word works? His Word is the same, yesterday, today, and forever, in every situation."

Martha finished her coffee. "Thank you for sharing, Anne. I really appreciate it." She sighed. "But truthfully, I was hoping to hear that you have a super secret picture of Irma with the quilt or something—something that would prove the quilt is yours."

"A secret picture?" Anne laughed. "Don't I wish? No, I'm afraid you'll have to figure this out the old-fashioned way."

Martha squeezed Anne's hand and then released it. "Well, if you run across anything that might help, please let us know. And I'll let you know about those letters very soon."

As Martha left the café, her thoughts were full of what Anne had said about filling the hole in her life with activity instead of people. As Aaron had done for Anne, Chuck had reminded Martha to take a breath and relax when she got fixated on what needed to be done. On warm evenings, he'd coax her to leave her to-do list and join him and the kids outside to catch lightning bugs or to lie on the grass and look at the stars. Then, after they tucked the kids in bed, he'd finish the supper dishes while she picked up the clutter from the day.

Thank You, Lord, for a man who helped me be a better person, and who let me know he was better because I was around. She chuckled to herself as she opened her car door. This gratitude thing really did work.

CHAPTER TWENTY-TWO

Elizabeth had an idea. The morning seemed to drag as she waited for Martha to come back from the coffee shop. Even though it was a beautiful day, people must have decided to do other things besides shop at Secondhand Blessings. They'd only had a handful of customers, and those were mostly tourists who bought small items as mementos of their time in Amish country. Elizabeth and Mary were both on their second muffin when Martha finally breezed through the door. Not that Martha ever breezed in and out of anywhere, Elizabeth grudgingly admitted to herself. Martha wouldn't stay away from the shop a minute longer than it took to talk to Anne. Now, Mary, on the other hand, was very breezy. No telling where the wind would take her and for how long.

Martha greeted her sisters as she came in the door. "Hey, you two. Did you manage to scrape along without me?" She looked at both of them and chuckled. "Do we suddenly get a muffin break in the middle of the morning?"

Mary swallowed her bite. "It's been really slow here. We're just taking sustenance before the madding crowd arrives."

"Um..." Martha hesitated. "Did either of you get anything done on my list?"

Mary rolled her eyes, and Elizabeth let out a groan. "No, we didn't work on the list. But I have an idea that I think will make up for it."

To her surprise, Martha didn't get upset by what surely she perceived as idleness on their part. Instead, she lifted her eyebrows and said, "What idea?"

Elizabeth rubbed her hands together. "It just occurred to me this morning that we've told Rachel about the quilt, but we haven't shown it to her. She's such a skilled quilt maker, I think she'd be able to tell us more about the quilt just by looking at the different stitching."

Mary jumped off her stool. "I think that's a marvelous idea. Let's call her."

Martha pointed at Elizabeth. "You're right. I hereby declare you absolved of all to-do list responsibility because of this brainstorm of yours. I'll give Rachel a call while I get lunch ready."

"Oh, great." Mary groaned. "So the responsibility is now all mine, huh? Is there anything I can do to get rid of it?"

"You can come help me with lunch," Martha said. "We'll eat sooner that way."

"I'm all for that," Mary said, following her out the door. "I think Elizabeth can handle things on her own for a bit."

Elizabeth waved them out and turned to survey the shop. I *couldn't handle this on my own,* she thought. Once again her heart filled with gratitude when she thought of her sisters and realized she didn't have to.

Martha entered the shop a half hour later to relieve Elizabeth, her arms full of the strawberry muffins she'd baked that morning. "Your lunch is on the stove," she said. "Mary is almost done eating, and she'll be here in a few minutes."

"Did you call Rachel?" Elizabeth asked.

"I did," Martha said. "She said she'd come by this afternoon. She has a couple of things she wants to show us, so it'll kill two birds with one stone."

After Elizabeth left, Martha got busy replenishing the display case. Mary arrived shortly after she'd finished with that task and retrieved Martha's to-do list from the bulletin board. "I'm going to show you I'm not completely lazy," she said to Martha. "I can get started on making sure we have all the puzzle and game pieces for the toys in the children's area."

Martha laughed. "I see you skipped right over cataloging the items that Della and the crew brought in this week." She laughed again when Mary stuck her tongue out. "I'm kidding. Let's get to work."

They continued to go through the list as the afternoon wore on. Elizabeth joined them, and they took turns waiting on customers. It had picked up a bit, something Mary noted out loud.

Martha was almost done washing the display glass window when Rachel came in the door with Dorcas and Hannah. Rachel was holding a large bag, and Hannah was carrying a basket. Rachel kissed the top of Dorcas's kapp and pointed her to the children's area. Then she and Hannah went to the counter where Elizabeth was checking out a customer.

Martha walked over to greet them. She gave Hannah a hug, then Rachel, and had them follow her to the back room, where she'd laid the quilt out on a table. Elizabeth joined them.

"Mary said she'd watch the shop and keep an eye on Dorcas as long as we tell her every single word that's said," she said.

"Thank you so much for coming by, Rachel," said Martha. "You said you have something to show us, so why don't you go first?"

Rachel put her bag down and pulled a wooden board from it. When she laid it on the table, Martha could see that it was a breadboard made for kneading dough. The board had a one-and-a-half-inch lip on it that would keep the board in place when jutted up against a countertop. The board itself was a work of art—maple inlaid with darker wood in an intricate shape of a maple tree.

Martha ran her hand over the satiny smooth finish. "Rachel, this is exquisite. Did Silas make it?"

"No," Rachel said. "Luke made this. He is seventeen now and has been working with wood for a few years. He has made many of these for our young friends who have married. When I was in here the other day I noticed that you do not have anything like this for sale, so I mentioned to Luke that I could show you one of his breadboards."

Martha clapped her hands together. "Rachel, it's gorgeous. I know the perfect place for it in the shop. Can Luke get us more like it?"

Rachel opened her bag again and took out two more boards. One was a darker wood with a lighter inlay, this time of a horse and buggy. The second was made to look as if it were made of building blocks, with almost a 3-D effect. Martha didn't know which one she was going to buy for herself, but she knew that very soon one of them would be on her kitchen counter.

Elizabeth turned to Rachel. "Please tell Luke that we'll take these and any others he'd like to sell. And if he has other items he makes, we'd love to see those as well." She laughed and jerked her thumb over her shoulder at Martha. "I can tell that Martha is already kneading bread on one of your boards. I can predict that one of these won't make it to the shop floor."

Martha grinned. "I can't deny it," she said. "When you're right, you're right."

Rachel nodded at Hannah, who took the dish towel off the top of her basket. Inside were rag dolls—Amish dolls—dressed in authentic Amish plainclothes. The women had white prayer kapps, long dark blue dresses, and snow-white aprons, and the men had dark blue shirts and black overalls. The men dolls wore the traditional Amish head covering—a wide-brimmed straw hat. There were smaller dolls that Martha assumed were children. They were dressed the same as the bigger dolls, except the girls had black prayer kapps. None of the dolls had faces, in keeping with the Amish tradition of not making any graven images.

"Ohhh," said Martha and Elizabeth together. Hannah took a doll from the basket and handed it to Martha.

"Hannah, did you make these?" asked Martha. She examined the stitching in the doll's apron and marveled at the young girl's skill. The stitches were tiny and evenly placed. Martha knew that if Hannah was the seamstress, Rachel had taught her well.

Hannah ducked her head modestly. "Yes," she said. "I was thinking maybe...if you think it would be okay...maybe you could try selling one in your shop?"

Martha looked at Elizabeth, who nodded eagerly. She turned back to Hannah. "Hannah, we would be so happy to sell these! I don't think you'd be able to keep up with the demand, though. We'll sell them as soon as they are put on the shelves, I'm sure."

"I can make more," Hannah said. "I finished school this spring, so I will have more time now to earn some money. Maam helped me think of something I could make that you didn't have yet."

Elizabeth had taken the doll from Martha, and now she put it back in the basket. "We'll take them all, and any more you make," she said. "Why don't you and I go find a place to display them, and we can discuss how much we should sell them for?"

Hannah followed Elizabeth back into the shop, and Martha took Rachel over to the table where the quilt was laid out.

"We were hoping maybe you could look at the quilt and see something we can't see," she began. "You know, any clues about the people who made it, if the skill levels are the same, that sort of thing."

Rachel bent over and peered at the quilt. "I can try." She ran her fingers over one square after another, slowly, examining the stitching carefully. Finally she straightened up. "It is surprising," she said. "I think you told me that the girls who made this quilt were thirteen years old?"

"Yes, that's right," Martha told her. "What's surprising?"

"Well, it is just that some of these squares look like they were made by a beginner, but then there are several others that are much better made. Here are two"—she pointed to two of the blocks—"which are exceptionally well done. I would say that these three were done by someone with decades of embroidery experience." She touched a third block. "And this one square looks as if two girls stitched it. The stitches are not alike."

"I don't know how that could be," said Martha. "We know that there were five girls in the circle, and they were all the same age."

Rachel touched her arm. "I am sorry that I was not able to help you."

Martha laughed. "No worries, Rachel. We like our mysteries to be very mysterious." She took Rachel's arm and pulled her toward the shop. "Now let's go find the perfect spot for *two* of Luke's breadboards."

CHAPTER TWENTY-THREE

L ater, at the tail end of supper, the phone rang, and Mary stood from the table to answer it. Martha went to the sink and started filling it to soak the silverware. She could hear Mary's side of the conversation over the running water.

"Hello? Oh, hi, Anne...No, it's not a bad time, we just finished supper....Well, I think we would love to. Let me ask the others." She put her hand over the receiver and turned to Martha at the sink and Elizabeth, who was stacking plates at the table. "Anne would like us to come to her house for a slice of cake this evening. Do you want to go?"

Martha turned the water off. "I'd like to," she said. "She told me this morning that Aaron's been gone for a few days to see his brother in Ohio. I think she's getting a bit lonely."

"Sounds good to me," said Elizabeth. "I'm always up for cake."

Mary returned to the phone call. "We'd love to come, Anne. How about if we come in about thirty minutes? That'll give us time to clean up our dishes.... Okay, see you soon, bye."

Twenty minutes later the sisters were in the car headed for Anne's house. Martha, as usual, was driving, and as she turned onto the street where Anne lived, she asked, "What are the chances Anne's made a chocolate cake? That's what I'm hoping for."

Mary raised her hand. "That's my vote! Chocolate chocolate chip with chocolate icing, and maybe chocolate syrup over it."

Elizabeth laughed. "You haven't changed a bit, Mary. Remember your sixth birthday party? You requested a chocolate cake with chocolate icing and chocolate ice cream with hot fudge and chocolate sprinkles, and chocolate milk to drink. You'd told all your first-grade girlfriends that the only gift you wanted for your birthday was chocolate, so you ended up with tons of candy bars and chocolate kisses."

"I remember that," said Martha. "Mary was sicker than a dog all that night. Are you sure it was her sixth birthday? I thought she was older than that."

"I'm sure," said Elizabeth, nodding. "I remember because I'd just turned thirteen, and my friends had all told me how chocolate caused acne. So I was scared to eat anything at the party." She crossed her fingers. "I'm hoping for Italian cream cake, but I'm not holding my breath. That's pretty much over the top."

They pulled into Anne's driveway and got out of the car. Anne and Aaron lived in a neat little ranch house with two towering maple trees on either side of the walk leading to the front door. A big picture window had drapes drawn across it, but they could see that the lights were on in the front room. Anne was opening the door before they reached the top step of the porch.

"I'm so glad you all could come," she said, taking Martha's elbow and ushering them inside the house. "Do you mind if we sit at the table in the kitchen? It's the coziest spot in the house, and I have enough Amish still in me to think of the kitchen as the heart of the home."

"You don't have to be Amish to believe that," said Elizabeth. "We really appreciate the invitation. And we're looking forward to your cake. I've tasted many of your creations over the years I've been back here. Mama always said no one could bake like Anne Hostetler."

Anne blushed. "That's so good of you to say. I hardly ever make cakes anymore, at least not for just Aaron and me. We can't afford to eat it all ourselves." She pulled a chair out from the table. "But please, sit down, and I'll serve you. Would you like milk or water with your cake? Or how about coffee? I have decaf."

Martha and Elizabeth chose decaf coffee, and Mary chose milk. They made small talk with Anne while she cut the cake. When she put the first piece on the table in front of Elizabeth, Mary caught Martha's eye, and Martha had a hard time not giggling. Chocolate cake with chocolate icing. Mary was in seventh heaven.

Halfway through their cake, the phone rang. "Oh, please excuse me," said Anne, rising from the table. "That might be Aaron, so I better answer it." She went to the phone where it sat on the counter and picked up the receiver. "Hello," she said. Then she didn't say anything for a few minutes—she just listened to whoever was talking on the other side.

Martha watched as Anne's face grew red. Who was it? What could they be saying to Anne that would upset her like this? Finally, Anne murmured, "I see. No, don't worry. I'm glad you called me. It's better to know about these things. Thank you, goodbye."

The three sisters watched Anne as she walked back to the table and sat down. Martha knew Elizabeth and Mary were as concerned as she was about the elderly woman. Mary, thank goodness, didn't stand on ceremony in the best of times, so it didn't surprise Martha when her youngest sister spoke up. "Anne, what's wrong? Who was that?"

Anne put her elbows on the table and laid her head in her hands. Elizabeth, who was closest to her, put her arm around Anne's shoulders and said, "Anne, we're here if you want to talk. Or if you don't, that's fine too."

Anne lifted her head, her eyes filled with tears. "That was my friend Susan Wright. She said that she was in the hardware store today and heard Betty Yoder talking to someone in the next aisle. She said Betty was saying I was a thief and only wanted the quilt because I wanted to sell it. She said Betty has been telling a lot of people that she wouldn't be surprised if it's not the first time I've taken something from the Amish and sold it."

Mary gasped. "Surely Betty isn't that mean-spirited. I know she's hurting over this quilt, but to accuse you like this...that's so wrong of her, no matter how she feels."

"What can we do for you?" Martha felt the need to do something, anything to help the woman who suddenly looked spent and exhausted.

"There's nothing." Anne shook her head. "I foolishly believed that at some time I would be able to have relationships with my friends and family again. But if this is what Betty thinks of me, I see there's no hope at all for that."

Elizabeth went to the sink and came back to the table with a glass of water. "Here you go."

Anne took the glass and sipped slowly. "Thank you."

"It's been like this since you left?" Martha tried to imagine the pain if former friends suddenly treated her as Betty had Anne, and then continued in that behavior for almost sixty years.

"It has." Anne looked at Martha with sorrow in her eyes. "It was very hard after Aaron and I left the church. At first, I tried to go home. It was too hard."

"Why?" Mary's brow furrowed as she listened with her unique intensity.

Anne patted her hand. "While my family would allow me to come, they wouldn't talk to me during meals—I couldn't even sit at the same table as they were. It was part of the shunning, letting me know I'd made the wrong choice." She shrugged, and sadness touched her features. "They couldn't understand that by choosing to live as an Englischer I wasn't choosing against them. That's how interactions with my family are to this day. It's like I exist, yet I don't. It's a hard place to live."

Mary leaned forward in her chair. "That's so sad."

"I should expect no more and no less from my former friend. A part of me wants to believe that at some point we could act civilly toward each other. But look at me, covered in wrinkles and with a crown of gray hair. If it hasn't happened by now, it never will." She sighed as another tear leaked down. "I am a fool to hope for anything to change."

Mary shook her head and edged closer. "We can always hope for that."

"True, but sometimes it is more fruitless than others. Change of the kind required is outside my control, and I had to relinquish my family and friends long ago. It is obvious Betty isn't willing to let go of the offense she believes Aaron and I committed when we left the Amish faith. It doesn't matter to Betty that I've been in church every Sunday since I left. All that matters to her is I left this community—left the Amish." She shrugged. "The irony is I have lived every day of my life within thirty miles of her. I've never left her."

Martha rubbed Anne's hand. "What can we do to help?" she asked again.

"Only the good Lord can change a heart," Anne said. Then she straightened, and a determined look came over her face. "Now, when I invited you here, it wasn't just for a bite of cake."

Martha looked at her, puzzled. "It wasn't?"

"No," Anne answered. "Today the Lord brought to my mind a box that's been in our attic for many years. Just before my mother died, she sent it to me, with a note telling me she wanted to remind me of my Amish roots. I keep that note on my nightstand, even after all these years. It was her way of letting me know she couldn't completely turn her back on me and that she still loved me." She got a faraway look in her eyes. "That was over twenty-five years ago. It's been a long time since I looked in that box, but maybe there's something about the quilt in there."

"Would you like our help to go through it?" Mary asked.

Anne thought for a moment. "No," she said at last. "I think I'd rather do it on my own. But if you could get it down from the attic for me, that would be most helpful."

Mary pushed to her feet. "Just tell me how to get there, and I'll have it down for you in a jiffy," she said.

Anne told her where the attic door was and how to lower the unfolding ladder that was built into it. "Aaron transferred the contents of the box to a plastic tote for me and then put 'From Mom' on it. It's a purple tote and should be easy to find."

Mary nodded. "I'm on it," she said. While she was gone, Martha and Elizabeth finished their cake and told Anne about the dolls that Hannah had brought into the shop.

Mary returned and placed the tote on the table. It was about the size of a large microwave, and Mary was huffing, so it was probably pretty heavy. Mary dusted her hands together. "Is this where you want it, Anne?"

"This is perfect." Anne ran her hand over the top of the tote. "I can sit here with a cup of tea and go through things at my own pace. Thank you, Mary. Oh, to be young again!"

Martha and Elizabeth both laughed. "Yes," Elizabeth said. "We all wish we were as young as our baby sister."

Mary grinned, sat down, and finished the last bite of her cake. Then she stood. "It's time for us to head home, I think."

Martha agreed. "Anne, thank you again for the delicious cake. And please, let us know if you want any moral support as you go through your box. We want to help you any way we can."

"Thank you, girls," Anne said. "I'll let you know as soon as I can if there's anything about the quilts or the circle in there."

"Who knows?" said Elizabeth. "You might find something that proves the quilt is yours."

"Or prove it's not mine," Anne said.

Martha could feel her pain. It bothered her to see Anne so burdened now. "It might have been better if the quilt had never appeared."

"Don't say that." Anne glanced at the tote, a quiet longing in her eyes. "It is a piece of someone's history. I hope it's mine, but it has value because of the hours of labor and love someone or a group poured into creating the blocks and then quilting them together. Come what may, I hope the answer is in my mother's things."

The car was quiet on the ride home. It wasn't until they were turning into their own drive that Elizabeth spoke. "Poor Anne. I can't even imagine Mama going one whole day without talking to me when we were together, much less a lifetime. What must that be like?"

"That's a question I hope I never know the answer to," said Martha as she parked the car. "I just hope Anne can find something in that box that will bring her family back to her somehow." She followed her sisters up the sidewalk to the house. *Thank You, Lord, that even though I didn't get to tell Chuck goodbye, I don't need a box to hold my memories of our times together. My heart is aching, but it's full of wonderful memories no one can take from me.*

CHAPTER TWENTY-FOUR

The next morning when Martha came down for breakfast, she found Mary in the kitchen ahead of her, pouring a cup of coffee. Mary handed her the cup and poured another for herself.

"What in the world are you doing up so early?" Martha asked her after her first sip.

"I dreamt last night about a quilt made of flowers, and I wanted to take a couple of hours before the shop opens and see if I can paint it." She gulped down her coffee. "You don't mind, do you?"

Martha started to assure her it was fine, but Mary went on without hardly taking a breath. "Oh, and Bill texted me last night. He wanted to know if I'd like to go with him to the Biblical Tabernacle at the Mennonite Center in Lancaster tomorrow afternoon, and then we'd meet you and Elizabeth for supper around six at the smorgasbord. I told him I thought that'd work for us. So ask Elizabeth and let me know, okay?"

She was gone in the next second, and Martha was left with her mouth open, clutching her mug. She chuckled and shook her head, recovering from Hurricane Mary. Elizabeth came in the kitchen, looking back over her shoulder at the living room.

"Was that Mary who just ran out the door?"

"Yes. She had an inspiration last night about a painting, and she can't wait to get it down on canvas. I expect we can count on opening the shop without her this morning."

"I think we can handle it for a couple of hours without too much trouble," Elizabeth said, taking another mug from the cupboard. "Besides, we know where to find her."

"She said something about us meeting her and Bill at the smorgasbord tomorrow night for supper. Do you want to? I guess it'd be about six, after we close up. They're going to the Tabernacle before that."

"I took Mama there a couple of years after Daddy died," Elizabeth said. "It's really something. You and I should go sometime. I think you'd enjoy it." She poured herself some coffee. "But yes, I'm fine with meeting them for supper. Do you think they'd mind if I invited John? I'd like him to be able to spend time with you and Mary, and I think he and Bill would hit it off."

"It's fine with me, and I don't think Bill or Mary would have any problem with it," said Martha, although the thought of being a fifth wheel was a little uncomfortable to her. "Do you think we'll hear from Anne soon?"

"I wouldn't count on it," warned Elizabeth. "When we left last night she seemed pretty wrung out, and who knows how she'll really feel about going through the box once she starts? I wouldn't be surprised if she just can't bring herself to get past taking the top off."

"Even if she does, there's no guarantee she'll find anything at all that will help us." Martha put the back of her hand to her forehead, sank dramatically into a kitchen chair, and said in her best southern belle accent, "I simply don't know how much more of this my little ol' detective brain can take, honey chile. I just can't think about it today. I'll think about it tomorrow."

Elizabeth grabbed a dish towel and started fanning Martha's face. "Don't go gettin' the vapors on me now, Scarlett." Laughing, she took the egg carton from the refrigerator. "How do you want your eggs this morning?"

Martha grinned. "Scrambled, my dear. Definitely scrambled."

When Elizabeth left the house at nine thirty to open the shop, she saw a car parked in the lot out front. "Who in the world—" she said out loud, stopping on the porch as the car door opened and someone climbed out. With a start of recognition, she opened the screen door of the house and called, "Martha, Anne is here." Then she rushed down from the porch as Anne came up the walk toward her.

Anne greeted her breathlessly. "Oh, Elizabeth, I hope you don't mind my showing up early like this. I thought maybe it would be best to see you before the store opens and you get busy. But I can wait if it's not a good time."

Elizabeth reached out and gave Anne a hug. "You're perfectly welcome anytime, Anne. Did you find something in the box?"

"I did," Anne said, excitement shining in her eyes. "And I just couldn't wait to show you."

"I told Martha you're here, so she should be coming soon." Elizabeth hooked Anne's elbow with her own and steered her toward the shop. "Let's get inside, and we can look at what you have before we open."

Elizabeth unlocked the barn door and led Anne to a stool behind the counter. "Let me get the lights on real quick— would you like a cup of coffee?"

"Yes, please," said Anne. "If you'll have one with me."

From the office where she prepared the coffee, Elizabeth heard the front door open and shut and then heard Martha's voice and Anne's response. "Good morning, Anne! How are you?"

"I'm a little tired, but I'm excited about showing you something I found. Elizabeth went to get us some coffee."

Elizabeth put a third pod in the machine and a moment later carried three mugs on a tray to the front of the shop where Martha was filling her display case with individually wrapped muffins and breads. "I brought you some too, Martha."

"Thank you, Lizzie." Martha picked up a mug and took a sip. "Ah. I'm really glad we added a coffee machine that makes individual cups quick. Sometimes you need a cup of coffee right *now*."

Anne picked up her mug. "Can I show you now?"

Elizabeth picked up her own mug. "Yes, please. I'm very curious to see what it could be."

Anne pulled two sheets of notepaper from her bag. "I didn't make it through the entire box last night. I only got about halfway. But I found this, and thought it might give some weight to my claim on the quilt." She held the papers out to Elizabeth.

Elizabeth took the papers from her. The one on top appeared to be a list of scripture verses. She recognized most of them. "These are the scriptures from the quilt, aren't they?"

"Yes," Anne said, her cheeks pink with excitement. "And read the note on the next page."

Elizabeth shuffled the pages and read the faded writing. "It's dated January 23, 1921, at the top, and it's from Irma, Anne's cousin. *'I've written down the verses you've each said you'd like to stitch. That way if one of us changes her mind and wants a different verse, she won't pick one that someone else is already doing. But if you choose a new one, let everyone know!'*"

Elizabeth looked up from the paper and met Anne's eager, shining eyes.

"What do you think, Elizabeth? Don't you think that proves that the quilt is mine? It seems as if Irma was the one who organized the girls. Why else would she do that if she wasn't the leader of the group?"

Martha took the papers from Elizabeth and studied them. Then she looked up at Elizabeth also. "It seems Anne has just as much claim to the quilt as Betty does. Betty has evidence that the quilt was Melinda's idea, and Anne has evidence that Irma was the leader of the group."

Elizabeth shook her head. "Oh, Anne. I wish I were Solomon and could split the quilt down the middle and satisfy both you and Betty. But I don't have the wisdom of Solomon, and I certainly don't know whose claim is the stronger one. I'm sorry this is so hard on both of you."

"I'll be all right." Anne took a deep breath, then set her mug on the counter. "I want the quilt to be mine, but maybe it isn't. Maybe this is all an effort to hang on to a piece of who I once was."

This quilt meant more to Anne than the fabric and stitches. And Elizabeth had sensed a similar intensity in Betty. This quilt represented much more to both women, yet both of them couldn't be the rightful owner. Other than being careful to treat each woman and her story with care and respect, Elizabeth was at a loss about what to do. Somehow, God would have to give them the wisdom to mediate this matter.

While it might seem like a small thing to some, she fully believed God cared, and He could and would help them. If He cared about the flowers and the birds, then He surely cared about what weighed on the hearts of His children.

Elizabeth pulled herself from her thoughts and turned to Anne. "Let's wait and see what else you might find in your mother's box."

Anne shrugged. "I was hoping that list and the note from Irma would settle the matter. But I'll finish looking through the box as soon as I get home and rest a bit."

But even as she said it, a sinking feeling came over Elizabeth. What if, after all this time, neither Anne nor Betty could prove the quilt was hers?

CHAPTER TWENTY-FIVE

Martha laid her hand on Anne's arm. "We need to finish opening up the store, but let me get you some more coffee, and we'll continue this discussion. I've just had an idea I'd like to explore." The more she thought about it, the more she thought it might just work.

Anne handed her mug to Martha. "Oh, don't you worry about me. I'm just fine sitting here and watching you two work."

Martha laughed and turned to go to the office. "Pretty soon I hope you'll see *three* of us working. Elizabeth, do you think Mary will be long?" she called. "I want her to hear my idea too."

She heard the front door of the shop open, and Elizabeth saying, "There you are. I thought you'd be longer with your painting. But let me tell you what Anne found—"

The coffee machine drowned out whatever Mary said in answer. A few minutes later, Martha carried two mugs out to the shop and handed one to Anne and one to her younger sister. "How did you get on with your painting?" she asked Mary.

Mary blew on her coffee. "It's not going to work. In my dream it looked fantastic—the colors, the textures, the blending of the flowers into one quilt." She waved her free hand. "But on the canvas...not so much. I guess I'll just have to keep dreaming."

"Did Elizabeth catch you up on what Anne showed us?" Martha asked her.

"She did. I came over to hug Anne and see the list and note for myself." Mary pointed to the papers on the counter.

Elizabeth approached the counter, dustrag in hand. "We're ready, and we have about ten minutes until opening. Who wants to split a cookie with me?"

Anne raised her hand. "I do. I've heard so much about Martha's cookies. Do you have any double-chocolate ones?"

Martha laughed. "You and Mary. I just baked those early this morning." She went behind the display case and took out two double-chocolate cookies. Elizabeth held out her hand for one, and Martha gave it to her. Elizabeth broke it in two and handed the larger piece to Anne. Martha broke her cookie in two and gave half to Mary.

"You know, circles were so common as I grew up." Anne's voice had a nostalgic ring to it. "There were circles for girls who shared the same birth month or the same favorite color. You might have distant cousins connected through a circle. I even heard of one that was based on where grandparents were from." She chuckled softly. "It really could be any reason or no reason."

"Were you part of one?" Martha leaned forward and tried to read the emotion in Anne's eyes. Was it too much to probe? She sensed that Anne would view the willing audience for her story as a gift.

"I never was." Anne sighed. "I wasn't one for staying indoors and writing letters. I preferred working in the garden or help-ing my brothers around the farm. When my mother didn't need me in the house, that is."

"I enjoyed reading the circle letters and getting that inside glimpse into what life was like then." Mary smiled softly as if she could see the letters and their content.

"I was surprised by how little life seems to have changed for the Amish." Martha felt her face redden when the others looked wonderingly at her, and rushed on, "I just mean I would have thought there would be more changes. I know they're Amish, but as much as everything else has changed, I just thought they would too. It must be really difficult to see change all around you and be able to stay the same."

"It is true that the world has moved forward with lightning speed. It's amazing how much change can take place in one lifetime." Anne shook her head. "Yet the Amish have managed to stop time to a large extent. It continues to impress me when young adults choose to stay after their rumspringas. But the simple life can be appealing."

"It's not for everyone." Mary patted Anne's knee.

Anne nodded. "No, it's not. I may miss elements of my family and old life, but I do not regret the choice I made. It was right and true for me." She sighed again. "I must release the hope that certain family and friends will ever understand that choice. It is all right. I've lived with it for more than sixty years." She laughed. "To think I've waited sixty years for some of them to change their minds. That is the definition of foolish and stubborn. Ah, well. Aaron and I have had a good life."

A tinge of grief squeezed Martha's heart, but just for a moment before she shook free. *Thank You, Lord, that Chuck and I had a good life. Like Anne, I have no regrets about the path we chose to walk together.* In no time, she would join Chuck in heaven. It might be years on this side of eternity, but she knew it would be a meaningless blink of the eye once she arrived.

Mary broke the silence. "How, exactly, did the circle letters work? Did each girl have a certain month to write her letter?"

"No, usually the way it worked was the first girl wrote a letter. She sent it to the next girl, who would read the first girl's letter, write her own letter, and send the two letters to the next girl, who would read the letters and add her own. It went that way, each girl reading the enclosed letters, and adding her own, until it came back around to the first girl. She would then take her original letter out of the envelope and write a new one, which she would add to the others and send to the second girl. So eventually everyone would get to read every letter."

"How clever!" said Elizabeth. "And so different. That would mean that each girl would be collecting and keeping her own letters instead of the other girls' letters." She frowned. "So why do the packets of letters we found have more than one girl's letters in them?"

"I think I can answer that," said Anne. "My older sister was in a letter-writing circle when I was little. She loved horses, and the girls in her circle shared her passion for them. They kept the circle going for years, but decided to stop when the last of them got married. My sister asked the others to bring their letters to the girl's wedding so they could divide them and have each other's letters for a memento. The girls in Irma's circle probably did the same thing at some point."

"I've loved the idea of letters traveling through a circle of friends ever since we discovered the first batch of letters. What a charming way to stay connected," Elizabeth said.

"I just wish they hadn't stopped writing," said romantic Mary. "Think of the fun we would have, reading about new babies, children growing up..."

Anne placed a comforting hand on Mary's shoulder. "All things run their course and then are over. Even good things." She turned back to Martha. "Now I want to hear this idea of yours."

Before Martha could respond, the shop door opened and several women entered, laughing and chatting.

"I'll help them," Mary said. "It's penance for getting out of opening this morning."

Elizabeth smiled at her. "We'll gladly let you," she said. "We'll fill you in when you get back." She turned and looked at Martha expectantly.

Martha took a deep breath. "I was just thinking. We've only been considering and thinking about Melinda and Irma, and whether they own the quilt. But there were five girls involved in the circle." She counted on her fingers. "Mildred Yoder, Irma Bontrager, Katie Filbrun, Pearl Beiler, and Hazel King. What if the quilt didn't belong to either Mildred or Irma? What if it was Hazel's? Or Pearl's? Or Katie's?"

Elizabeth stared at Martha, her mouth open. Then she nodded. "You're right. We've been so fixated on Mildred and Irma that we haven't even considered the other three. But how would we even go about finding them? All we have, essentially, are their first names. I'm assuming odds are that they were all married and changed their last names."

"Elementary, my dear Elizabeth. Old-fashioned hard work. Asking more questions. Maybe Rachel could help us. I just wish we had more than their names and ages in 1920 to go off of."

"As far as we know, they all lived in Pennsylvania," Elizabeth said. "That's a start, anyway."

Martha tapped her fingers on the counter. "And Pennsylvania is filled with Beilers, Kings, and Yoders." She sighed. "Well, I'll see what Fanny Fraser can do. She might know of some census data that will help us trace at least a couple of them through time. Elizabeth, either you or Mary could go talk to Betty and see if she can think of anything at all that would help us find these girls."

"What will we do if you do find them?" Elizabeth frowned. "They have to all be dead."

Martha laughed. "Well, of course they're dead. I mean we might be able to find a younger relative, a niece or nephew like Anne or Betty who remembers the quilt." Martha could feel the challenges exploding in her mind. "It might be a dead end, but at least we'll know we tried."

"So we have a plan?" Elizabeth finished her cookie and brushed the crumbs from her fingers.

"We do," said Martha firmly. "Tomorrow, while you and Mary hold down the fort and talk to Betty, I'll go to the library and talk to Fanny."

Anne slowly pushed to her feet. "And I'll think about those girls. See if I remember anything about them as women." She waited a moment, as if waiting for her balance to catch up with her. "I'll leave you girls. I've taken enough of your time for one day."

Martha walked Anne to her car. "Thanks for coming this morning and showing us that list, Anne. You've been so helpful and understanding through this whole conundrum."

"I'm not done yet," Anne declared. "I'll let you know if I find anything else in the box."

Martha helped her into her car, shut the door, and waved her off. She felt like she was in some cosmic game of Hot and Cold. Were they getting closer to the solution to the mystery or moving further away?

CHAPTER TWENTY-SIX

Martha had settled onto the couch with a mug of tea and the TV tuned to a sappy movie on one of the cable channels she rarely watched. It was another one of those movies where ultimately you knew the guy would get the girl, but Martha really didn't want to think hard. The burden of the quilt felt heavier than it should. After all, it was just fabric stitched together with a little thread...and a lot of love. *Father, will You help us figure it out? I know it may seem like a small issue, but to Anne and Betty it's not.*

And Martha felt the burden to do right by both women. She was coming to understand that what the quilt represented mattered significantly to both women. They weren't trying to be difficult. They simply wanted to hang on to their past and good memories.

She pulled a small afghan from the back of the couch and tugged it over her legs. The colors formed a rainbow, and she smiled as she remembered her mother crocheting it on that very couch, using the leftover yarn from the baby blankets she routinely crocheted for a local crisis pregnancy center. Her mother had delighted in that act of service. How many nights had she spent happily settled in the very place that Martha now filled, crocheting an endless supply of blankets?

She shook off her thoughts and picked up the letters that were lying on the couch beside her. She'd gone through them carefully, trying to get a feel for the personality of each girl. They were, each of them, delightful thirteen-year-olds.

Hazel King lived in New Holland and seemed like a sweet, yet spunky girl. She loved all things domestic and helped care for her younger siblings. She enjoyed cooking and baking and serving others, and dreamed of the day she would have her own household. She'd already named the eight children she was sure she would have.

There were two girls from Lancaster. Irma Bontrager's letter hinted at her insecurities. Thirteen was a hard year no matter when you lived. You stood on the cusp of womanhood, but were still more child than adult. Standing betwixt and between and wondering where you fit. As the youngest in her family, her parents would have been older, and probably not as active as they once were with her older siblings. Martha chuckled, remembering Mary's laments through her early teen years about how Mama and Daddy didn't want to get out and "do things" like they used to.

Pearl Beiler, who lived in Strasburg, had a quiet strength that was reflected in her letters. She wrote about the same hardships that Mildred had—the drought and shortage of food—but she also wrote about her little brother's illness and how they feared for his life at one point. Pearl stayed at her brother's side many nights, giving him sips of water, wiping his fevered brow. Martha assumed Jacob pulled through, since Pearl didn't say otherwise in her later letters.

Katie Filbrun, from East Petersburg, wrote with loopy letters and little caricatures decorating the edges of her pages. Her words were simple, but direct. She took joy in the antics of her animals. She barely mentioned her siblings, instead spending her words on tales of the adventures her pets enjoyed, including the cow with the artful tongue. Her letters reminded Martha of books like *The Cricket in Times Square* or *Charlotte's Web*. Simple stories that gave her animals, and there were many, life and dimension.

Then, of course, there was Melinda Yoder, Betty's aunt, and the other girl from Lancaster. Martha knew Melinda was the oldest of many brothers and sisters, some, like Betty, much younger than herself. She supposed that position in the family, plus the hard times she'd written about, must have caused her to grow up faster than some of the other girls in the circle.

Martha settled back and rubbed her eyes. She looked at her watch. How had she spent over an hour reading through the letters? She knew the girls in the circle better, but had it moved her closer to knowing who had sewn the quilt?

Mary walked in holding Tinkerbelle, with Pal at her heels. "How's the movie?"

Mary's question startled Martha. "I'm not really sure. I haven't paid much attention."

"Background noise."

"Something like that."

"I can't stop thinking about Anne and Betty and that quilt. Who knew something like that could cause such conflict?"

Martha tugged the blanket a little closer as Mary sat next to her. Tinkerbelle squirmed free and edged onto the blanket, and Martha scratched the dog's ears. "I keep wondering how the two families could have the same quilt."

"Me too." Mary sighed. "So how do we solve this puzzle?"

"Carefully." Elizabeth's voice pulled Martha's attention toward the living room's doorway.

"Let's give it a couple more days." As Martha turned to look at Mary, her younger sister shrugged. "What will it hurt? Nobody's going anywhere. It's not like we're in a hurry."

Martha saw her point. "Okay."

Elizabeth nodded. "I'm good with that. It'll be sad for one of the women to be disappointed, but there's only one quilt. Tomorrow I'll visit Betty and ask her to check with other family members."

Mary held up her hand, causing Martha to chuckle. "I can chat with Anne."

Martha turned off the TV. "All right. That leaves me with trying to track down some of the other circle girls. Maybe I'll start at the library."

"That's a great idea, Martha," Elizabeth said. "And we can all ask God to direct our efforts."

Martha smiled. "That's an even better idea. After all, it's no mystery to Him whose quilt it is."

The next morning Martha was waiting at the library when the doors opened. Fanny had her hair pulled back in one braid rather than her usual two. Her eyes also looked weary as she smiled while clutching a mug of something steaming.

"Good morning, Martha. Can I help you with something today?"

Martha nodded. "I've got a list of girls who were thirteen in 1920. They were all local Amish, but I need to see if I can find out what happened to them."

"Really?" Fanny's eyebrows wrinkled, and her mouth puckered as she looked at Martha. "Why do you need to find them? You know they probably aren't living anymore."

"I know." Martha sighed as the enormity of the task overwhelmed her. "We're still trying to figure out something about a quilt we're selling. These girls were all involved in the same circle, and I'm hoping I can find a relative who might be able to help us know more about it."

"A sticky problem?"

"You could say that."

"Related to the one you were in for earlier?"

"Yes. And thanks again for your help with that one. You went above and beyond, which made me think if anyone can help us, it's you."

Fanny set her mug down, and her gaze roved over the stacks of books. Martha could almost see her mentally scanning as her gaze traveled, as if looking for the right place to start. "You're wanting to do more genealogical research then, rather than historical research. This will be different than digging back through newspapers on microfiche."

"True, and I'm just as clueless about how to do it." Martha pushed a strand of her hair behind her ear, feeling how much she didn't know. "Maybe I should have researched first, since I don't even know what to ask."

"No, that's what I'm here for. I actually took a class on this kind of research in college. It's a prime activity at libraries. We pay the subscription fee as part of our operating expenses." She tapped her chin, then nodded. "All right. We're going to start with census data."

Fanny stepped from behind the desk and led Martha to a small room set to the side of the main library room. "This space is primarily for genealogical research. We have a couple of computers set up just for this work. One of the things to keep in mind is that there is a '72-year-rule' that affects all census records. It's a federal law that prohibits any release of individual census data until seventy-two years have passed. So any records past 1946 haven't been released yet. You shouldn't have any trouble accessing 1920 data though."

"That's so interesting, especially that they chose such a specific number."

Fanny's face lit up, and Martha could tell that she was a born librarian. "I know, right? I would assume it's because back when the law was enacted, the average lifespan was about seventy-two years, so they must have figured that the person whose information would be released would probably be dead by the end of the time limit and it wouldn't matter anymore." She moved a computer mouse and woke up one of the computers. "In England, they have the same type of rule, but it's for one hundred years."

Martha laughed. "Those Brits must live cleaner than us Yanks." She sat down at the computer. "What am I looking for?"

"It really depends on what you want to know. You know the girls you're looking for were thirteen in 1920. You can look in that year's records and see if you can find their households. Then you could look in later years and see if they're still listed in the same household or not. If they aren't, that would probably either mean they married or died. But in the end, it's probably a pretty fruitless way of going about finding out, because there could be many people with the same names, so unless you know their family members' names, you'll just be guessing if you have the right record or not."

As Fanny kept talking and showing her online resources, Martha realized it was going to take hours of work to find who these girls became as women. And that was if she could find the right records. The census pages were handwritten, and scanned into the database.

"Do you have the girls' addresses?"

Martha gazed at the computer screen, feeling a daze of overwhelmed anxiety. "Only one of them—the one I don't need. Melinda Yoder from Lancaster. She's Betty Yoder's aunt, so we know where her relatives are. Well, I don't need Irma Bontrager's address either. She's Anne Hostetler's cousin, and we know her married name is Troyer. We didn't find any envelopes addressed to the girls. I know what towns they live in because they talked about that in their letters, but I don't have specific addresses, no."

Fanny groaned, and the bell over the library's door rang. "Well, why don't you get started while I see if this patron needs help? I'll check on you periodically, or you can come find me if you have specific questions. I would start with one or two of the names and see what you can find. Use them as practice runs. At least you have the city to go on with them."

"Sounds good." Martha turned her attention to the census documents and, out of curiosity, decided to see how hard it would be to find Melinda Yoder in Lancaster in the 1920 census at Hattie's address. Her heart dropped as she clicked through page after page of census documents. It would take days to look through all of them. It felt like she was digging through an enormous haystack looking for a very tiny needle.

She hoped it wouldn't be that way once she got to the smaller towns the other girls were from. She brought up the pages for the 1920 census of East Petersburg and found Katie Filbrun after a few minutes. Her father was Levi, forty-eight years old, and her mother was Sarah, forty-six years old. She had a small family, as Amish go, with no brothers and only two younger sisters, and they lived on a farm market road. Martha wrote down the details and was excited until she realized afresh that it didn't do her much good to know these facts if she didn't know what family Katie married into. Oh, why couldn't Amish boys write letters and quilt? Martha puffed out a chuckle at her thought and kept clicking.

Since she'd had a bit of success with Katie, she decided to try the other two girls who were from a smaller town. It didn't take her too long to find Pearl's household in Strasburg, and Hazel's in New Holland. She congratulated herself and wrote down the data for all three girls, because, well, you never knew, did you?

CHAPTER TWENTY-SEVEN

The house smelled of fresh-baked muffins and something sweet and spicy when Elizabeth made her way downstairs. She'd somehow slept right through Reddy's alarm, and the house was quiet. Had Martha already finished her baking and left for the library? As Elizabeth glanced at the clock and noted it was after nine, she decided that was probably very likely.

Martha wasn't one to let any moss grow beneath her, so chances were she had waited at the library for the building to open. That left Elizabeth to find Mary and coordinate who would work at Secondhand Blessings when it opened while the other went to talk to Betty.

Elizabeth did not relish the thought of going to Betty, who'd been so certain the quilt was hers, and telling her they still weren't sure. She could imagine how well that conversation would go.

She sighed as she went to the coffeemaker and brewed a cup of coffee into a mug that said on one side, "I smile because you're my sister," and on the other side, "I laugh because there's nothing you can do about it." Mary had gotten that cup for Martha, and it always made Elizabeth smile. After eating one of the muffins Martha had left on the counter, she hustled outside to find Mary. Her little sister was coming toward the house with a basketful of eggs. "I went ahead and fed the inside animals and cleaned the kitchen. It was clear you needed the sleep."

"You didn't have to do my chores, but I appreciate it."

"It's my pleasure to serve you." Mary grinned her way with that annoying kid-sister glimmer. "You can pay me back next winter when it's below freezing and the snow drifts over our boots."

Elizabeth laughed. "How about if we both open the shop and see what kind of morning we have? If it's slow I'll run on out to Betty's."

"It should be slow this morning," said Mary. "Remember, there's that big craft show in town from nine to one, so we won't get busy until this afternoon. When you get back, I'd like to run over to Anne's. Martha made that list of the girls' names and where they're from, and I'd like to run them by Anne, see if any of them ring a bell. Then I need to leave this afternoon about three, but Martha will be back by then. Bill is picking me up to go to the Biblical Tabernacle. Did you call John like you said you were going to?"

"I did. He's going to pick Martha and me up, and we'll meet you and Bill at the smorgasbord at six."

"Excellent. Bill will call ahead for a table. It's Saturday night, so they'll be busy. I'm really looking forward to it." Mary waved as she walked toward the house with her basket.

Thirty minutes later, Elizabeth was in the car driving to Betty's house. The azaleas were showing the effects of their lifespan, a few lonely blooms hanging on, but most having already fallen off. The screen door didn't open before she could reach the porch this time. Instead, she had to rap on the door several times and was glancing around to see if she'd missed Betty in the yard when the door finally opened.

Betty's kapp was perched precariously on top of her head, and she didn't have the carefully pressed air that usually followed her. Instead, she looked worn down, with bags under her eyes and more pronounced lines on her face.

"Betty, are you all right?"

"Ne." She sighed and stepped back from the door. "You may come in."

"Thank you." Elizabeth opened the screen door and followed Betty inside.

"You have come to tell me that I cannot have the quilt." The words were a firm, sad statement.

"No, I came to tell you we still aren't sure." Elizabeth pulled a chair from the table. "Let's sit down."

After they were seated, Elizabeth took a deep breath. "Betty, Anne showed us a letter yesterday. It was one of the circle letters, and it was from her cousin, Irma."

"And?"

"It had a list of the scripture verses that the girls stitched for the quilt. Anne is thinking maybe that might mean that Irma was the leader of the group, and therefore the letter may be more evidence that the quilt belongs in her family."

Her words made Betty sit up straight. "So you are going to let her buy it?"

"No," said Elizabeth. "We still have more questions that we need to find the answers to." She told Betty about Martha's theory that they might find out more if they pursued information about the other three girls in the group.

"Because it doesn't seem like it's either yours or Anne's," she concluded. "Obviously, the girls made the quilt together. So how do we go about knowing who assembled it?"

Betty frowned at her. "And how did they decide who got to keep the quilt?"

"That's what we don't know." Elizabeth shook her head and then glanced down at her hands. "Betty, what if we find out that it belonged to one of the other girls in the circle? Are you okay with not receiving the quilt? With us deciding that it's not yours and possibly not Anne's either?"

"As long as it does not go to her." The woman practically spit the last word.

This was clearly more than a competition for ownership of pieces of fabric. "Betty, why are you holding on to such animosity toward Anne?"

"She left us."

"And she's sorry to have hurt those she loves, but still feels she made the right choice." Elizabeth held up a hand to stop Betty. "You can't control her heart and decisions. She has a right to decide how her life will go."

"But not when I loved him too." Betty clapped a hand over her mouth and looked as if she wanted to call back the words.

"Oh, Betty. I'm so sorry."

"It was a long time ago." Betty sniffed as if it didn't matter, but Elizabeth could see that it did. "Anne was two years older and snagged Aaron's attention. I thought I had a chance, but I was a fool. And then, she lured him to leave the church. If he had married me, he would never have left the church. He would be able to see his family, and he would be happier."

"When Anne told us about leaving the church, she said it was something Aaron wanted too."

"Of course she would say that." Betty buried her face in her hands. "I have never told anyone this."

No wonder it had caused such resentment. "Something like that can eat us alive if we don't tell someone. I'm so sorry you've carried this alone for so long."

"Fifty-six years." Her laugh wasn't joy-filled, but tinged with bitterness.

Elizabeth's heart broke for the older woman. She thought of her own single life and God's protection that kept her from marrying a man she'd thought would love her but later proved to be unfaithful. It had been a trying time coming to a place where she was comfortable and content with her role as the elder sister who returned home and cared for her elderly parents.

Maybe Betty felt some of that angst.

"Can we pray about this together?"

"No, thank you. God has left me alone for this long. I attend services, but He showed He was uninterested in me long ago."

"Betty, that's not true. He's always there if we'll just turn to Him."

"Maybe so, but I am not interested today."

"That's all right. But I will pray for you often. Anne longs for your friendship." Elizabeth pressed out a sigh. "Does she know?"

"I did not tell her." Betty straightened her shoulders and raised her chin. "And I trust that you will not tell her either."

"Would it bother you if I told my sisters? You can trust the three of us to keep it secret. It would help them understand why you feel so strongly about the quilt not going to Anne."

Betty hesitated. Then she slowly nodded. "You may tell your sisters. But no one else."

"Thank you," said Elizabeth. "Now, if you could talk to your family, see if someone else remembers the quilt."

Betty stood. "I will ask around. But for now I must get to work."

Elizabeth rose with her. "Thank you for your time, Betty. I will be praying for you. We truly want to make sure the quilt goes where it should."

"It will not be easy to reach them all."

"Try the ones you can. Any bit helps. Also, have you thought more about who was in the circle? Can you give us any more information about any of the girls?"

"It was before my time, and Aenti Melinda would simply say that she and a group of her friends worked together and sent the letters." She walked Elizabeth to the door.

Elizabeth gave the prickly lady a hug and felt her relax, just a bit. "Thank you for sharing your story."

"Remember it is mine and not yours."

Elizabeth paused long enough for Betty to meet her gaze. "I will honor your story. Anne won't hear about it from me."

CHAPTER TWENTY-EIGHT

A nne moved back to the small red-and-chrome kitchen table, coffeepot in hand. As Mary smiled her thanks for the fresh coffee, she knew they could sell the table, matching vinyl chairs, and most of what was in the room as shabby chic or vintage and charge a pretty penny. The room looked like something out of a *Leave It to Beaver* episode, and it was charming.

"Aaron will be back from Ohio the middle of next week." Anne brushed her hands against her apron. "This old place gets lonely when he's gone. It might be why I stayed so long at Secondhand Blessings yesterday. I'm sorry about that."

"We enjoyed spending time with you." Mary reached across the table and patted Anne's wrinkled hand. "We appreciate your bringing the list of quilt scriptures."

"I only wish it had been more helpful." Anne pushed to her feet and headed to the refrigerator. "I forgot to offer you cream. I have one of the fancy flavored ones, and good old-fashioned cream from a cow."

Mary held up her cup. "I would love some straight from the cow."

"Oh, Betsy's not in here." Anne winked, and Mary caught a glimpse of the playful woman she remembered as a teen. "But I'll be glad to serve her good cream."

"You own a cow?"

"Oh no. The last thing Aaron and I need to do is care for one of those mammoth creatures. My son keeps a couple. Every week he brings us fresh milk and cream. I like to make butter with it, but I always make sure to save back enough cream for cooking and coffee." Anne offered Mary a charming small pitcher shaped like a cow, and Mary tipped the tail up until the cream dribbled into her mug.

Anne put a teaspoon of sugar into her own coffee. "Although I'm always glad to see you girls, I'll admit I'm not sure why you're here."

"Martha went through the letters again last night. I was just thinking, if you knew where the girls were from, maybe you might remember something Irma might have mentioned." Mary recited the names and the towns. "Do any of those names and places sound familiar to you?"

Anne frowned as she considered. "I don't know. Can you tell me again? Slowly."

"Hazel King?" Mary said the name, then paused. "She was from New Holland."

"I knew a Hazel King, but that was her married name."

"That wouldn't be the right one then." Mary said the next name. "How about Katie Filbrun, from East Petersburg?"

Anne sighed as she rubbed her forehead. "I just don't know."

"How about Pearl Beiler from Strasburg?"

"Do you have any idea what any of these girls' married names were?"

"Not of those three. Of course, Melinda Yoder never married, and you told us Irma's married name is Troyer. Martha is working on the other three at the library. Otherwise, we're at a loss. We almost have to stumble on a relative or close family friend."

Anne rested her coffee mug on the table. "I remember when Irma got married there was a family that came from East Petersburg for the wedding. I don't know if it was the same family." Her eyes got a faraway look. "I remember the woman brought Irma the most beautiful quilt, and then, later, when Irma had her first son, she sent her a gorgeous baby quilt...."

Mary picked up her mug and took a sip of her coffee. "There are so many questions about the quilt. It seems each time we learn something, it only opens the door for more questions rather than answering any."

Anne eased to her feet and then waved for Mary to follow her. "I just thought of something that might help, but you'll have to assist me."

Mary followed her down a short hallway that dead-ended at a bathroom door with a bedroom on each side. The wallpaper was a faded floral pattern, and the carpet under their feet was a clean but well-used shag green that had been fashionable decades earlier. They entered a small bedroom on the left that looked like it was used as a guest space. A double bed was covered with a beautiful wedding ring quilt, with small wooden bedside tables on both sides. A matching dresser sat against a wall between two windows.

Anne led Mary to the closet and slid one of the pocket doors to the side. She pointed to a box on the shelf. "If you can get that down, inside are some of Irma's things, including that baby quilt. I'm not even sure how I ended up with it, but I did. Maybe we'll find a clue inside."

"I suppose it's possible." Mary had to reach on tiptoe, and even then wasn't quite tall enough. "Let me get a chair."

"There's a chair in the other bedroom. Aaron doesn't like it if I climb on things anymore. I tell him he's too worried about nothing."

"Better safe than sorry." Mary grabbed the chair from the room across the hall and placed it in front of the open closet. A moment later, she had tugged the box free and stepped off the chair. "Where would you like me to set it?"

"Right here on the bed is fine. I haven't thought about that box in years."

Mary set the box on the bed, then stepped back so Anne could open it.

Anne tugged at a flap and then eagerly pushed the other three aside as she pulled out a layer of tissue paper. "I hope this helped keep the dust out." She tossed the paper on the floor and then paused before looking inside. "This feels like an adventure."

"I love your enthusiasm."

Anne grinned at her, then turned and looked inside. She paused as her hands caressed something. Mary leaned over, and her breath caught. "Is this what I think it is?"

"It's the baby quilt the woman from East Petersburg made for Irma."

Mary leaned back as Anne tugged out the small quilt that had a Bible verse embroidered across the top. "'Thou wilt keep him in perfect peace, whose mind is stayed on thee.' Isn't that from Isaiah?"

"Isaiah 26:3. Irma always said a baby needed to be wrapped in perfect peace."

"It's true." Mary ran a light hand over the top of the fabric. "It's so soft."

"I can't believe I've forgotten about it all these years." Anne set the quilt to the side and reached back in. "Let's see what else is in here." She pulled out a small wooden box, about the size of a cigar box. It was obviously handmade, with colorful flowers stenciled on the lid. Inside were what looked to be about a dozen intricately stitched handkerchiefs, all folded and pressed into perfect squares.

Mary was so impressed by the box, she almost forgot that they were looking for clues. Then Anne reached to the bottom of the box and brought out a pile of yellowed papers.

"Do you think these may be part of the circle letters?" Anne handed the ribbon-tied bundle of letters to Mary. "I'd like you to read them and see if they help."

"I can do that right now."

"No, take them home and share them with your sisters. You know they'll want to read them too." Anne glanced at the letters, and a sheen of moisture came to her eyes. "My cousin was an amazing woman. So godly and kind. She loved everyone well. I've always wanted to be like her. I hope you find something meaningful in the letters."

"I promise I'll treat them with great care."

"I have no fear that you would treat them otherwise."

Mary glanced at the bedside clock. "Oh my. How did so much time get by? I'd better get back to the shop. Elizabeth will have my guts for garters."

"Thank you so much for coming to see me." Anne led the way back to the small living room.

"It's my pleasure." Mary gave Anne a quick hug.

After they finished their goodbyes, Mary hurried to her car. She couldn't wait to get back to her sisters with the letters. If they were fortunate, those letters would have a key to unlock the quilts. If not, they would be at least interesting. The innocent perspective of the other letters had been refreshing to read in the modern world that tended toward jadedness.

She grinned in anticipation of what they might find. What secrets could these new letters hold?

CHAPTER TWENTY-NINE

After a couple of hours spent hunched over the computer at the library, Martha's brain had turned to mush. She had nothing but the three addresses and family members' names of the girls from the smaller towns to show for her efforts. She was just about to gather her belongings when Fanny came back.

"I'm sorry I haven't been able to check on you until now. Things got crazy out there, but it is Saturday, so I'm not totally surprised." She sat down beside Martha. "Have you had any success?"

"Not really." Martha sighed. "I did find the other three girls' addresses in the small towns they lived in."

"Well, that's something, isn't it?" asked Fanny.

"I don't know what good it does me," said Martha. "Even if I have their addresses, they would have moved out of their homes when they married, and I don't know their married last names to know where to look for them. I'm right back where I started."

"Oh." Fanny looked as downhearted as Martha felt.

"I was laughing at myself, thinking that it would be so much better if these were boys I was searching for, and then their names would stay— " She cut herself short as an idea began to take root.

Fanny laughed. "I bet Amish women wished sometimes that their sons made quilts too." She looked closer at Martha. "What's wrong?"

"I think I have an idea." Martha whirled back to the computer screen. "What if..." She brought up the census report for New Holland for 1940 and scrolled through the pages. "I'm looking for Hazel King's name—yup, here's her father and mother again, at the same address. But no Hazel."

She quickly pulled up the 1940 census report for East Petersburg and began scrolling through the pages of hand-written documents.

Fanny was bouncing on her seat in impatience. "What? What are you looking for?"

Martha scrolled over the names. "Bingo!" she all but yelled.

Fanny gripped Martha's hand, stilling the mouse and getting her attention.

"It came to me when I thought about how boys don't change their names when they marry. And what do we know about Amish men? What happens when their parents get older?"

"Sometimes a man will move into his parents' house with his family and build a dawdy haus for his mom and dad on the property."

"Yes," said Martha. "And if the mom and dad have no sons? Then what can happen?"

"Well," said Fanny, "then I suppose one of the daughters can move into the family house with her husband and family. The mom and dad would still go to the dawdy haus."

"Exactly!" Martha pointed at her. "So if the oldest daughter, in this case, Katie Filbrun, gets married and moves into her parents' home so they can go to the dawdy haus, then she'll be listed by her married name as living at that address!"

"Brilliant!" Fanny yelped. She held her hand up for Martha to high-five, and Martha did.

"See here." Martha pointed to the screen. "Here's the same address, and here's a Katie *Lapp*, and also listed are Levi and Sarah Filbrun."

"Try the last one," Fanny urged.

Martha changed to the 1940 Strasburg census and scanned the pages. "Pearl's family must have moved," she said. "There's another family living at that address." She checked the 1920 census report for Strasburg and got the same result.

Martha stood and gave Fanny a hug. "Thank you so much for your help."

"My help?" Fanny snorted. "You didn't need my help. You came up with that bit of genius all on your own."

As soon as Martha got back to the house, she grabbed her pad of notes and headed across the yard to the barn. A couple of cars were parked out front, but when she entered, Elizabeth was waiting as two couples browsed in different areas.

Martha still had a rush of pleasure when she saw people coming to Secondhand Blessings. Life had taken such an unexpected turn, but it was one she was enjoying.

Elizabeth waved her over. "Learn anything good at the library?"

"Not until the very end. I'll save the story for supper tonight at the smorgasbord." She glanced around. "Where's Mary?"

"She went to ask Anne about the circle girls, to see if she could recall anything about them if she knew where they were from. She should be back before too long."

Martha rubbed her hands together. "Boy, when it rains, it pours, doesn't it? We're getting close, I can just feel it."

Elizabeth hurried to the house to make some sandwiches for them. After she returned and they'd eaten, Martha went through a couple of boxes of items a woman had dropped off for possible consignment. There were some records that could sell well if the right person wanted them. Maybe Martha should find a site to list them on online. She could see a collector snatching up the entire collection since the albums were in remarkably pristine condition. She couldn't find any scratches on any of them.

She returned to the front of the shop and between customers tidied up some of the display tables. The whole time her mind spun trying to put the pieces together. The story of the crazy quilt was slowly revealing itself. A mystery that had to be teased out thread by thread, but in the end would be a beautiful tapestry that told the story of young girls who had come together to share life almost a hundred years earlier. She tried to think what the equivalent would be today, but an email thread didn't even come close to having the same weight and permanence as the letters sent so long ago—the paper yellowed and the ink faded but the words still true.

A middle-aged couple had come in while she was working. The woman stopped beside a table and tugged her husband back. "Stephen, this looks just like my grandma's quilt."

Martha glanced at the table and groaned. What was the quilt doing out on the sales floor? Had Elizabeth or Mary gotten it out and forgotten to put it away? Now the woman was looking at it, a smile lighting up her face.

"I think I've told you about it."

The man had a receding hairline and trim figure. He glanced at the quilt, then at his wife. "If you say so."

She laughed and patted his shoulder. "I should have known it wouldn't register for you. My grandma loved to tell the story of how she was a part of a group of girls who sent letters to each other, kind of like a round robin. You would add to the letter and then take out your part when it got back to you and replace it with an update."

"You mean people used to send letters?" His words were teasing, but his wife ignored them.

Martha headed toward them and noted Elizabeth doing the same from her station at the counter.

"I remember her telling me about a scripture quilt."

Martha stopped across the table from them. "I'm sorry, I couldn't help but overhear. Are you saying you recognize this quilt?"

"Well, I don't know if it's the same quilt. I just remember my grandma talking about making one. She said something about each girl making squares with scripture verses on them."

Elizabeth edged into the group and extended her hand. "I'm Elizabeth Classen, and this is my sister Martha Watts. When did she make the quilt?"

The woman brushed a strand of hair behind her ear. "Grandma Katie didn't mention specifics that I remember. I do remember she loved it though."

Martha froze. "Katie?"

"Yes." The woman looked puzzled.

"Was her name Katie Lapp?"

The woman stared at her. "Why, yes. That was her name."

"And her maiden name was Filbrun?"

"I don't know. Her daughter was my stepmother, and I don't remember ever hearing what Grandma Katie's maiden name was."

Martha smiled. "We've been tracing the history of this quilt. It's good to know another piece of it." She ran her hand over the quilt. "Do you know if your grandmother was the owner of the quilt? Did she give it away or sell it, do you know?"

The woman's expression dimmed, and she shook her head. "I don't remember her ever saying. I just remember how much she loved the quilt and what it meant to her. It would really surprise me if she gave it away or sold it."

"Do you mind if we get your names, just in case we have questions?" Elizabeth reached into her pocket and pulled out a scrap of paper and stubby pencil.

"Not at all. I'm Charlotte Hawkins, and this is my husband, Stephen."

Elizabeth jotted the information down and then took their contact information. "Thank you."

Martha grinned at her sister as the couple left the shop. "It's looking more and more like the girls shared the quilt." She spread her arms wide. "Who'd have guessed a clue would just walk in the door like that?"

CHAPTER THIRTY

Martha was folding up the quilt when Mary returned a few minutes later.

"Uh-oh. Did I forget to put that away?"

Martha looked up from her careful folds. "Yes, but it turns out it was a good thing. That couple that just left recognized it."

Mary stopped dead in her tracks. "Really? What happened?"

"A coincidence that wasn't a coincidence, that's what. Katie Filbrun's granddaughter was just here."

Mary turned back to the door. "I would have loved to hear what she knew."

"Not much other than she remembers her grandma talking about making squares for a scripture quilt."

"Wow." Mary clasped her hands and pulled them under her chin. "It feels like we're getting close."

Martha smiled. "That's what I said. It sure does." She turned to the counter. "If you're here, I'll check on the baked goods."

"Wait!" Mary said. "Don't you want to hear about my time with Anne?"

"I do." Martha looked around the shop and saw there were only two customers, regulars that came every Saturday and browsed through their new acquisitions. They were self-sufficient, and usually it was at least an hour before they were ready to check out. Martha called Elizabeth over, and Mary pulled a rubber-banded bundle from her bag. A familiar starry-eyed look came over her face as she held them.

"Anne remembered there was a box that she'd gotten of Irma's things long ago. You should have seen what was in it! There was this wooden box—I wish I knew who painted it— there were gorgeous flowers on the top, and there was this amazing baby quilt. You should see it—it's the softest material you've ever touched, and it's mint green and pastel yellow and cream—"

"Mary!" Elizabeth and Martha said together.

Mary blinked. "What?"

"What are those?" Martha pointed to the bundle.

"Oh, right." Mary handed the bundle to Elizabeth. "Anyway, at the bottom of the box was another bunch of letters. Anne said we could look through them and see what we can find."

Elizabeth tucked the letters into her apron pocket. "We'll have to save these until tomorrow, though. We're going out tonight, remember."

Martha pointed at Mary. "So Mary got the letters." She pointed to herself. "And I found out Katie's married name"— she raised her hand at Elizabeth's coming question—"I can tell you how at supper tonight." Then she pointed to Elizabeth. "What did you find out from your time with Betty?"

Elizabeth frowned. "I didn't learn much. Just that Betty was in love with Anne's husband."

Martha's mouth fell open, and she couldn't quite close it. "Did I just hear you right? Betty was in love with Aaron Hostetler?"

Elizabeth nodded. "But before Anne and Aaron married. It explains so much."

"Sure does." The lingering animosity on Betty's side made sense now. Her heart had been broken and never healed. "That's pretty sad."

"But Betty says no one knows, and we're not to tell. We have to keep it between the three of us."

Mary mimed locking her lips. "I won't say a word."

The shop door opened, and Rachel entered along with Phoebe. Phoebe had her basket over her arm, but she put it down on the counter and ran over to the three sisters. She hugged each of them and then stood patting Mary's arm, content just to be with them.

Rachel followed Phoebe more sedately, and Martha gave her a hug. "I didn't expect to see you today."

Their Amish friend was wearing a forest-green dress under her snowy-white apron. "I wanted to stop and learn if your searches have been productive."

Martha nodded. "Anne found more letters from our circle girls." Funny, they really did feel like her girls as she read the stories of their day-to-day lives and challenges. The fact the events had happened almost one hundred years earlier hardly mattered in a community like Bird-in-Hand, where so many still lived without modern conveniences.

While Elizabeth went to the cash register to help a customer, Martha asked, "Rachel, did you know a Katie Lapp from East Petersburg?"

"Katie Lapp? Why?"

"That's the married name of Katie Filbrun, one of the circle girls. At least that's what the 1940 census indicates."

"How old would she have been in 1940?"

"Thirty-three."

"So she would have been in her sixties when I was young."

Martha nodded. "That sounds right."

"Ja. There was a Katie Lapp in East Petersburg. She was a widow. She had two children, but I don't think they're still near here. I can ask my mother and some of her friends. What should I ask them?"

Martha straightened a stack of magazines on the table nearest her. "Ask them if they remember a quilt like the one we have, or if they remember Katie talking about any of her friends who might have made it with her."

"I will do my best." Rachel smiled at the sisters and took Phoebe's arm. "I will see what I can learn at services tomorrow."

As soon as Rachel and Phoebe had left, Elizabeth said, "I'll take the dairy basket to the house."

"Not so fast, missy." Mary leaned against the table and crossed her arms. "You need to explain the little bombshell you threw out before Rachel walked in."

"You mean Betty being in love with Aaron Hostetler?"

"Yeah, that one." Martha felt her heart tighten at the pain Betty must have felt. "She never did get married, did she?"

"She didn't." Elizabeth crossed her arms. "And she thinks that leaving the church was Anne's idea, and she was a seductive temptress to get Aaron away too."

Martha shook her head as she continued to straighten the items on the table. They really needed to get display racks for the magazines. "I wonder which bothers Betty the most. That Anne left the church, or that she ended up with the man Betty loved? My bet is on the love part."

"Well, either way, the one her animosity hurts the most is herself," Elizabeth said. "From what I can tell, she's pretty lonely. And the quilt seems to be bringing out these feelings in her even more. When I saw her this morning, she looked ill."

"The sooner we can solve this quilt mystery the better," Martha said. "For everyone concerned."

CHAPTER THIRTY-ONE

The rest of the afternoon went quickly, especially after Bill picked up Mary at three. The Saturday afternoon rush kicked in at the same time, and before Martha knew it, it was closing time. She and Elizabeth had just enough time to hurry to the house and get freshened up before John was at the door.

Elizabeth and Martha kept the conversation in the car light, talking mostly about Martha's children and grandchildren and John's son and daughter. Both his son and daughter had one of the steady summer jobs that came with living in a northern tourist area.

When they arrived at the Bird-in-Hand Family Restaurant & Smorgasbord, Martha marveled again at how much things had changed in the town. She remembered coming to the Bird-in-Hand Family Restaurant when she was young. Back then, it was a gray brick building with a gray mansard roof and had only a couple of windows to let in the sunlight. The building had been updated to red brick, with gable roofs, numerous large windows, and a bell cupola. They'd added a buffet, and most recently, a live theater featuring musicals and magic shows throughout the seasons.

Mary and Bill were waiting for them at a table in the large open dining room. After greeting them and taking her seat,

Martha picked up her menu. "How was the Tabernacle? I've heard people in the shop talking about it. It sounds really impressive."

"It was amazing," said Mary. "Everything is an exact replica of what's described in the Bible—the measurements of the courtyard, everything. It really makes the Bible come alive."

Bill picked up his own menu. "First they give about a fifteen-minute presentation of the history of the tabernacle, what was happening with the Israelites, and all that, and then they take you on a tour. Our guide really knew what she was talking about. Nobody could ask a question that stumped her." He grinned. "Believe me, I tried."

Mary rolled her eyes. "He really did." Then she laughed. "But I think she enjoyed the challenge."

Martha straightened her silverware. "Could you go into the tabernacle?"

Mary nodded. "All except for the Holy of Holies. They have a window you can look through to see the ark of the covenant and the wax figure high priest. Everything is so well done."

John opened his menu. "Can we have dessert first? I've been thinking about their red velvet whoopie pies all day."

Bill laughed. "Not me. I'm a shoo-fly pie man all the way. But I like the dessert first idea."

It didn't take long for everyone to decide that the smorgasbord was the way to go, and a few minutes later, they were seated with their full plates. Their server brought their teas and waters and sodas, and they tucked into eating. As they ate, the sisters caught the men up on the quilt mystery—leaving out the Betty/Aaron/Anne angle, of course.

Bill put his fork down. "So let me get this straight. There are five girls, and they each decide to make three quilt squares, each with a different scripture verse on them. But there's only one quilt. So they had to have sent the squares to one of them to assemble the quilt, right?"

"That's what we think," said Elizabeth. "At first we thought the one whose idea it was to make the quilt should have owner-ship, but then we thought it should be the person who was the leader of the group. Then we thought maybe the owner is the one who sewed the squares into a quilt. You can see our dilemma."

"And there's always the possibility that they got together at some point—at a social or a celebration of some kind—and all of them made the squares into a quilt together." Martha sighed. "We have one question. 'Whose quilt is it?' But we have too many answers."

John came back from his second trip to the buffet. "That letter-writing circle you talked about reminds me of something my sister and her friends did one summer." He asked Martha to pass the ketchup and poured it on his meatloaf. "They decided it would save time if they used carbon paper to write letters to each other. I think there were about six of them. So my sister would use four sheets of carbon paper, write her let-ter, and end up with five copies, which she'd then send to her five friends. Of course, the one who got the last copy some-times had to work to make out the words, especially if it was an old piece of carbon paper." He laughed. "It seems so old school now, doesn't it? But they thought it was the greatest idea since the record player."

Martha felt the same spark in her brain that she felt when she thought of the dawdy haus theory in the library. Something was right there...on the edge...aha! "Of course!" she cried.

"What? What?" echoed around the table.

"Carbon copies," she said. "What if each girl made three different scripture squares, but she made those three squares five times? What if they all made the same quilt with the exact same verses? Then they sent them with their letters, and each girl ended up with fifteen squares, ready to be assembled into her own scripture quilt."

Mary leaned forward. "So that would mean that the quilt we have could belong to any one of the five girls?"

"All this time," Elizabeth said, "we've been tearing our hair out, wondering how in the world both Betty and Anne could remember the same quilt in their family, thinking one of them must be mistaken, when they were both right!"

"But wouldn't it be too much to make five squares all the same? I mean, wouldn't that be...tedious?" Mary looked absolutely horrified at the thought of doing the same thing five times over.

"Not if you're a quilter," said Martha. "Quilters sometimes make the same square many more times than that. And I'm sure the girls' mothers agreed that stitching the same verse five times would be great practice."

Elizabeth waved her hand. "And—it would make each quilt unique in another way. No girl would get the first attempt of each verse for her quilt, and no girl would get the fifth attempt—and presumably, the most well-done—of each verse either. They would each get all levels of progress in the squares sent to them."

"But remember what Rachel said." Martha held up her finger. "She said there were two squares that looked like they were done by someone with decades of experience, and one done by two girls. What's that all about?"

John and Bill had been looking from one sister to the other as they threw out their theories. Now they looked at each other. "Did you follow all that, Bill?" asked John.

"I'm not sure," Bill said. "Have they solved it or not?"

John shrugged. "I have no idea. I'm not fluent in the sister language."

"Oh, no," said Martha, shaking her head vehemently. "We haven't solved it yet. Now we know why both Betty and Anne think this particular quilt is theirs, but we're no closer to knowing whose it is." She sat back in her chair. "A minute ago we didn't know what to do with one quilt and two people. How in the world are we going to deal with five quilts and their ensuing complications?"

After supper Mary and Bill decided to take in a movie in Lancaster, so John took Elizabeth and Martha back to the house. Elizabeth asked him to stay for a bit, and the two of them sat on the front porch in the twilight. Martha could hear their muffled voices as she put together a chicken casserole for Sunday dinner. She'd just put foil wrap on top of the pan and slid it into the refrigerator when she heard John's car drive off and Elizabeth come through the front door.

Martha shut the refrigerator door as her sister came into the kitchen. "I had a nice time at the restaurant. John and Bill know so many of the same people, I'm amazed they didn't know each other until tonight."

"John said the same thing," Elizabeth said. "I'm glad you came—in the first place, of course, because I like being with you—but also because otherwise you wouldn't have figured out the quilt thing. It all makes much more sense now, doesn't it?"

"It does," Martha said. "We were so fixated on there only being one quilt, we didn't even consider any other possibilities. Talk about getting tunnel vision." She wiped her hands on her apron. "Would you please give Betty a call and tell her our thoughts about there being more than one quilt? It's too late to call Anne. I know she goes to bed early."

While Martha finished up in the kitchen, Elizabeth took her cell phone from her bag and dialed Betty. "Hi, Betty, this is Elizabeth. I'm sorry to miss you. Listen, we're thinking now that the circle girls made enough squares for them all to make identical quilts. Well, not identical, they would have different backgrounds and borders, obviously. Anyway, could you ask your family about that? Maybe it would jog someone's memory. Thank you, we'll talk to you soon."

Elizabeth hung up. "Tomorrow afternoon let's go through Anne's letters and see if we can get any more clues. Now that we know there are five quilts, we might interpret something a little differently."

Martha hung the dishrag on the sink. "Sounds good to me."

"What sounds good to me," Elizabeth said, yawning, "is going to bed with a good book and reading until I fall asleep."

"I'll second that," said Martha, turning out the kitchen overhead light. "I'll leave a light on for the young whippersnapper with all the energy." She flipped the switch that turned on the light over the sink and took Elizabeth's arm. "Let's see if between us we old-timers can make it up the stairs."

CHAPTER THIRTY-TWO

After church the next morning, Martha got her casserole out of the fridge and into the oven. The service hadn't been easy for her to sit through. She'd tried to be grateful during the past week or so for Chuck's life, and it had helped remind her how blessed she was. But there was still the empty, unfulfilled feeling she just couldn't shake. *Just stay busy and get through tomorrow,* she told herself.

A few minutes later, she heard Elizabeth talking to Anne on the phone in the living room. Martha lost the conversation because she was setting the table and clinking plates and silverware, but it wasn't long before Elizabeth came into the kitchen.

"Anne says she'll ask her nieces and nephews about the quilt again, now that she knows there's possibly more than one."

"Won't it be uncomfortable for her to do that? I thought they weren't speaking to her."

"It's all right. She said the awkwardness has eased some over time. She's also going to check with her siblings and some cousins. She's half afraid one of them will have Melinda's quilt, and she'll feel foolish."

"We can only hope that both Betty and Anne will feel a little foolish when this is over, if that's what it takes for them to make amends." Martha grinned at Elizabeth and finished setting the table.

After dinner, Mary insisted that, before they looked at Anne's letters, she wanted to make a mind map—whatever that was—of what they'd learned about the quilt and the girls. So, while she worked on that, Martha busied herself in the kitchen baking for the shop, and Elizabeth went for a walk with Pal following her down the rural roads. When she returned she helped Martha in the kitchen. The kitchen was warm and smelled of divine spices, but Martha wondered if she'd ever get a sense of how many of each treat to bake. Demand for the pastries was still highly variable, and part of her liked that, because she didn't want to bake all day. However, when they ran out of muffins or scones an hour after Secondhand Blessings opened, she felt the missed opportunity and revenue.

Martha and Elizabeth were taking a break when Mary walked in carrying a large poster board. It looked like she'd taped several smaller ones together. Martha poured herself some more coffee while she watched Mary tape the poster to one of the kitchen walls, Mary had put the five girls' names in a circle like a string of pearls. Then she'd drawn connections between them and made notes about each. It was an interesting way to look at the information, and Martha studied it while she sipped her coffee.

Elizabeth refilled her own coffee cup. "So what's this called again?"

"It's a mind map." Mary put another piece of tape on a corner that kept popping up.

Martha squinted at the poster. "How did you learn to do this?"

"I don't really know." Mary washed her hands and took a mug from the cupboard. "I must have seen it somewhere. One of the groups I volunteered with or something like that." Mary looked at it and smiled. "It helps me organize my brain—no comment from the peanut gallery, please."

Martha grinned. "I'll control myself, although you're just begging for a sarcastic comment." She stood up and moved closer to the poster. "But this is impressive," she said. "It's a great way to see what we know."

Mary had also drawn another section with the quilt, the scripture verses, and what they'd learned from Anne and Betty about it.

The phone rang, and Martha picked up the cordless receiver Elizabeth had brought into the kitchen. "Hello?"

A very quiet voice answered. "Is this Martha?"

"Yes," Martha said. She frowned. "Betty? Is that you?"

"It is," Betty answered. "I know it is Sunday afternoon, and your day to rest, but I was hoping that maybe I could come there to talk to you all. I—I need to say something."

"Of course you can come, Betty. But I think it might be better if we came to you. Would that be all right?" She looked at her sisters and raised her eyebrows. Both Elizabeth and Mary nodded.

"Oh, could you? That would be so kind. Please do not hurry, if you have something else you need to do first. I will be here."

"We'll be there soon. Please don't worry about coffee or anything like that. We just had some, and we will just come to talk." She finished the conversation, assuring Betty it was no trouble for them to come, and hung up.

Elizabeth looked at her with wide eyes. "I wonder what in the world could be so important. Do you think it's about the quilt?"

"I don't know what else it would be about," said Mary.

Martha started for the stairs. "I need to get cleaned up a bit before we go. I'll be ready in twenty minutes."

Thirty minutes later, they were sitting at Betty's kitchen table, sipping from the mugs of coffee she'd insisted on serving them. Elizabeth looked at Betty, sitting between herself and Martha, looking like a shadow of herself as she stirred a spoonful of sugar into her mug. She wasn't sure how to open the conversation, because Betty seemed far away.

Betty looked at Elizabeth. "It has been very hard for me to sleep since you were here."

Elizabeth reached out and touched Betty's hand. "I'm sorry."

"Do not be sorry. Our conversation has made me think about many things." She sighed and seemed to shrink. "It was easy to pretend I had done nothing wrong when I could hide the darkness in my heart from myself. I could keep the focus on what I believed Anne did to me."

Martha sighed. "Hurts are hard to let go of."

"It is true. I have let the bad thoughts and feelings fester for too long."

Martha took ahold of Betty's other hand. "God can touch them at any time."

"I know. It is the letting go that is hard." Betty looked at her mug. "I have harbored them for many more years than I have not."

Mary smiled. "Then it's a good day for freedom."

"Freedom." The word brought a look of hope to Betty's face. "I have wondered what that would feel like."

"Maybe today you can start," Elizabeth said.

"How?"

"Forgive yourself and then forgive Anne and Aaron. While they may not have done anything wrong, to you it feels as if they did. I've learned it's a good idea to forgive people whether they need it or not. Whether they ask for it or not." Elizabeth placed a hand on her heart. "It does something inside me, even if I never tell them what or why I'm forgiving." She let the words sink in a moment. "At the end of his life our father had some trying times. He wanted so much to do all the things he'd done before but simply couldn't. That meant that he would get frustrated, and would often take it out on the people closest to him."

"It happens often with the elderly." Betty nodded knowingly.

"I know, but that didn't make it easier. I wanted to remember my father as he was. The man who had always been so strong. He provided so well for us, and then it was my turn to care for him, even if I couldn't be around twenty-four/seven. I wanted the service to be easy." Elizabeth shook her head. "Life had made things so I was the one to help my parents, especially my mother. It was a privilege, it was, but it was also a chore, and

I struggled sometimes not to resent it. But I soon realized that my bitterness was impacting no one but me."

"Your parents probably did not notice."

"I think our mother did. She was always sensitive to the hurts and concerns of others. She told me she prayed constantly for my heart. It always sounded strange, but now I realize what a gift that was. Our father didn't necessarily understand how caring for him and my mother impacted me. But my mother? She understood."

Martha looked at Elizabeth, her eyes filled with tears. "Oh, Lizzie. I know it was hard on you. So many times I've wished I'd helped you more, encouraged you more—"

"I've felt the same way," said Mary, her own eyes wet.

Elizabeth smiled, looking from one sister to the other. "You two were there when you could be, and I know that. I didn't always feel that way, but that didn't make it any less true. I don't wish for one day less with Mama and Daddy. Most of the time I feel sorry for you two that you missed out on those days." She laughed. "So don't go feelin' guilty on me."

Betty took a sip of her coffee and then studied Elizabeth. "It is hard to know how to forgive. How do I forgive myself for clinging to bitterness so long?"

"I think it's the same way we forgive others. We say the words, and then we ask God to do the work in our hearts."

"I should be dispensing wisdom to you, not the other way around." Betty paused, and Elizabeth gave her space to think. "I want to forgive Anne and get rid of this bitterness. I think my pride was wounded when Aaron made it clear I could never have him because Anne had captured his heart."

Together the four of them clasped hands and prayed, and Elizabeth sensed the sweet presence of God at that small, battered kitchen table. He'd met them just as He promised in the Bible. When they were done, a new light was in Betty's eyes.

"I do feel free."

"I'm so glad," Elizabeth said. "Are you ready to talk to Anne?"

"I think I would like to," Betty said. "Do you think one of you could be with me when I do? Or..." She looked hopefully at them. "Maybe all three of you?"

Martha laughed. "What if we had you and Anne to tea? Would that work for you to reconcile with her?"

Betty looked troubled. "Reconcile?" she said. "That word sounds too ambitious a goal after all this time."

"But you and Anne getting together would be a step in the right direction. Isn't that what you want?" Elizabeth asked. "To heal the brokenness between the two of you?"

"I am not sure that is possible, but I would like to have the opportunity to tell Anne I am sorry."

"We'll make sure it's a convenient time for Anne." Elizabeth had a feeling Anne would make time to heal the rift with Betty. "And I'll come get you and bring you home again."

"All right." Betty played with her kapp string. "I also need to tell you something that will make my actions the last two weeks look very foolish."

"What's that?"

"My sister-in-law has had Aenti Melinda's quilt all along."

The sisters looked at each other, openmouthed with astonishment.

"I listened to your message on my machine this morning. So I asked my sister-in-law, Ruth, at church about it, and she knew immediately what I needed to know. I have not spent much time with Ruth since my brother died. That is why I did not know she had it in her home." Betty sighed. "I have done a good job of holding myself away from others. If I did not, I would have talked to Ruth about the quilt sooner."

"Maybe that will change now too. By allowing God to help you forgive Anne, He can also heal the other relationships that have been strained." Elizabeth took Betty's hand again. "You'll see that people can be trusted."

"Maybe." Betty smiled, and her whole demeanor changed.

The women left with the promise that they would let Betty know when Anne could come for tea. Elizabeth was eager to set in motion plans for reconciliation between the two women.

Martha backed the car from Betty's driveway and started home. "Well, I guess that means I can honor my promise to Anne, and she can buy the quilt," she said. "I suppose it's possible this particular quilt isn't hers, but no one else has come forward claiming it, so I think our decision is made for us."

Elizabeth looked out the window at the buggies with families coming home from church or going off to visit relatives and friends. "I guess that's what it's coming down to." She took a deep breath. "But I have a feeling it's just not going to be that easy."

CHAPTER THIRTY-THREE

When they got back to the house, Martha followed her sisters in the door. "Did we hear back from the Hawkinses yesterday?"

Elizabeth shook her head. "We didn't. I have their number, but I don't want them to feel like we're badgering them."

"Maybe they'll call today. Chances are they got busy with their plans yesterday, but they seemed like the kind of people who would do what they said." At least Martha hoped they would, because if they could find Katie Lapp's quilt, it would narrow the field of those who might have owned the quilt that waited in their shop.

The phone rang as they entered the kitchen and Martha picked it up, saying, "Maybe that's them now." But it was Anne, wanting to stop by and see them for a few minutes. Martha told her, of course, she was welcome. When she hung up, she smiled ruefully at Elizabeth, who was taking a pitcher of iced tea from the fridge. "When did we get to be so popular?"

Martha laughed. "We do seem to be in great demand today, don't we?"

"I'm glad," Mary said. "I can't wait to find out if she can come tomorrow to meet with Betty."

Ten minutes later Anne knocked on the door. Martha hurried to greet her and give her a hug. "Come into the kitchen for a muffin and some tea."

Martha ushered Anne into the kitchen, where Elizabeth was arranging some muffins on a plate and Mary was setting the table with small plates and knives. Mary put the ice tray down and gave Anne a hug. "Would you like iced tea or hot tea? We have both ready, so either is fine."

"Is one of them decaf?" asked Anne. "It's getting late for this old woman to be drinking caffeine."

Elizabeth put the plate of muffins on the table and took a mug from the cupboard. "Hot tea it is," she said. "We have several different kinds of decaf tea, so that's no problem at all." She transferred their basket of tea bags from the counter to the table and received her hug from Anne.

Martha pulled a chair from the table for Anne and helped her pick out her tea bag.

"Are these Martha's delicious muffins?" Anne pulled the plate a bit closer to herself and examined the variety of treats.

"They certainly are," said Mary. She placed three more mugs of hot water on the table. "There's orange cranberry, poppy seed, and strawberry. We have plenty of all three, so you can try all of them if you want."

The sisters joined Anne at the table, prepared their tea, and chose their muffins.

Anne took a sip of her tea. "Thank you so much for letting me come on a moment's notice. I was coming home from a meeting at church, and you're on my way."

"Visiting with good friends is the best way to spend a Sunday afternoon," Martha assured her. "We're anxious to hear what you have to tell us."

"I talked to one of my sisters last night. She's almost ninety, but sharp as a tack. She mentioned something I'd forgotten."

"What's that?"

"As we talked about the quilt, she reminded me of a time forty years ago when people were breaking into Amish homes and stealing quilts. I asked her if that had happened to us."

Elizabeth paused, her muffin halfway to her mouth. "And?"

"Well, she said Grace's home was broken into." Anne pulled her muffin apart and spread some butter on it. "It was a long time ago, but Olivia said several quilts were stolen." Martha opened her mouth, but Anne held up a hand. "I asked about the one Irma made. Olivia wasn't sure it was one of the ones that was taken, but she wasn't sure it wasn't either. She said it could have been. I have a niece who likes to collect the family archives, so to speak. I've left a message for her."

Martha remembered what Rachel had said. "I wonder if Grace's family was at a funeral when the thieves broke in."

"I've tried to think back, but our family is large. And I was shunned by then, so if it was a cousin or aunt or uncle, I might not have been told." A flicker of grief crossed Anne's face, then she straightened. "Well then. No use wasting time feeling sad about something I can't control."

Martha looked at her sisters and smiled. "We have some good news for you about that, Anne," she said. "We saw Betty today, and..." She paused dramatically. "She'd like to meet with you to ask you to forgive her."

Anne's eyes went wide, and she looked from one sister to the other, dumbstruck.

Mary laughed. "Anne, say something!" she urged.

The elderly woman's eyes filled with tears. She grabbed Martha's hand and squeezed. "Betty? Betty Yoder? Wants to ask me to forgive her?"

Martha nodded. "She does."

Elizabeth had tears on her cheeks. "We'd like you both to come to tea sometime, Anne. Please say you will."

Anne's laughter shone through her tears. "Oh, I will," she said. "I want to see her as soon as I can."

Elizabeth frowned. "I hate to be the one to say it, but how will we have a tea when we have the shop to run?"

Martha saw Anne's shoulders slump. She thought quickly. "Elizabeth, we could do a breakfast tea, couldn't we? Tomorrow morning? Maybe around eight thirty?"

Elizabeth nodded slowly. "I think that would work." She turned to Anne. "Anne, would that be all right with you?"

Anne's face was wreathed in smiles as she nodded vigorously.

Elizabeth stood. "I'll go call Betty and see if that's okay with her."

Anne wiped her eyes with her napkin as Elizabeth went into the living room. "I've waited so many years for this day."

"I don't know how you've done it," said Mary. "I don't know if I could have kept myself from holding a grudge all these years."

"We must choose to love regardless of the pain," Anne said. "And always remember that God's love knows no limits. Even when we make our love conditional, His never is."

Martha patted Anne's hand. "That's good wisdom."

"Simply one of the benefits of this white hair."

Elizabeth came back into the kitchen and took her place at the table again. "Betty said the sooner the better. So we're on for eight thirty tomorrow morning."

Martha turned to Anne. "Another piece of good news is that Betty's sister-in-law has had her quilt this whole time. We know that the quilt we have isn't hers."

Once again, Anne's mouth dropped open. After a moment, she shook her head and chuckled. "I hope that's the last piece of good news. I don't know how many more shocks this old heart can take."

The women finished their muffins and tea through their laughter and tears. Finally, Anne ate the last bite of her muffin. "Martha, your muffins are perfection." She brushed crumbs from her fingers. "I must get home and call Aaron and tell him about all of this. I'll let you know if I hear anything from my niece about the quilt."

After Anne left, Elizabeth cleared the table while Mary ran some dishwater. Martha put on her apron to start baking for the tea. "Well, I guess we'll have to skip reading the letters tonight if we have a breakfast tea to get ready for," she said.

Elizabeth put the dirty dishes on the counter by the sink and gently took Martha's arm. "Martha, we haven't forgotten what tomorrow is. Remember, I asked you if there was anything special you wanted to do for it? I'm sorry we're adding more to your day with this tea."

Mary turned and put her hand on Martha's other arm. "I've been thinking about it too, wondering what we can do to make it easier for you."

Martha felt her eyes fill up with tears. "You two are the best sisters anybody could ever have." She wiped her eyes. "I don't think I could have dreamed up something more special than Betty and Anne putting old hurts behind them. I think it'll do me good to see grudges die and forgiveness asked for and granted." She rubbed her hands together. "Now, we have a lot of work to do. Who'd like me to make a list?"

CHAPTER THIRTY-FOUR

A couple of hours later the three women sat around the kitchen table to a supper of gourmet grilled cheese and tomato soup. Elizabeth had made her sandwich the traditional way, Martha's with pesto and tomato, and Mary's with gouda and bacon. Elizabeth considered with amusement how the different sandwiches reflected the different personalities of the sisters. She was the dependable eldest sister. Martha, the middle sister, had a bit of independent flair. And Mary was the zesty and unique baby of the family, always marching to her own beat.

"I love the idea of the tea for Betty and Anne." Martha dipped her spoon into her soup. "When I make scones and muffins for the shop, I'm going to make some smaller ones just for them."

"I'll run to the store in the morning early and get some fresh fruit." Mary dabbed her mouth with a napkin. "Should I make a salad, or just serve it cut up? Oh, and I'd love to make some cookies."

"Either way would be fine," Elizabeth said, "but what really matters is giving them some time and a place to talk." The thought made her heart warm. What would happen when the women arrived? All she and her sisters could do was set the stage for them to take the steps toward each other that they knew Anne wanted and that it looked like Betty was ready to take.

The sisters made a few more plans for the tea and then went about the tasks Martha had written up for them. After several months of life with her sisters, Elizabeth had settled into the reality that Martha would be the planner, and that was good. Her organizational skills kept them all on track. Elizabeth knew, though, that she'd have to find ways to remind her younger sister that life should be more than work. And Mary would keep them focused on people. Together, they'd be a team that built on the success of Secondhand Blessings.

As soon as the supper dishes were cleared, Martha whirled into action whipping up a batch of scones and another one of muffins. To think Betty was willing to close the gap that had festered all these years! It was hard to admit when you were wrong, and the more time that passed, the harder it was.

She'd just put the last tray of muffins in the oven when she heard her cell phone ring. She wiped her hands on her apron, grabbed her purse where she'd hung it on the back of a kitchen chair, and pulled her phone from it. The number wasn't one she recognized. "Hello?"

"Hello? Is this Martha Watts? This is Charlotte Hawkins."

"Oh, hello. How are you?"

"We're fine, thanks. Listen, I got a chance to ask my stepmother about the quilt last night."

"That's wonderful. Does she remember anything?"

"She does, actually. She said that her mother, Katie—whose maiden name was Filbrun, by the way—made the quilt, just like I told you. My stepmother has the quilt in a cedar chest in her bedroom. She was so surprised to hear that I saw one in your shop, and she wanted to know if you would send her a picture of it."

"I can do that," Martha said. "Is this your cell phone number? I could text the picture to you and you could forward it to her."

"Yes," Charlotte said. "This is my cell number. I would really appreciate it."

"It's no problem," Martha told her. "We appreciate your finding out about your grandmother Katie's quilt. Thank you for checking for us." After she hung up, Martha scrolled through her gallery for a picture of the quilt. She'd taken several on one of the days they'd laid it out in the shop. She sent the pictures to Charlotte, then put her phone away and studied Mary's mind map. Then she grabbed a pencil from the junk drawer and put a check by Melinda's and Katie's names. They knew where those quilts were.

The landline phone rang as she was staring at the drawing, and she picked up the handset. "Hello?"

"This is Anne. Are you Martha?"

Martha smiled at the way Anne had phrased the question. "I am. Weren't you just here?" She chuckled.

"Wouldn't you know that while I was at your house my second cousin left a message on my answering machine? Irma's quilt landed on her side of the family." Anne chuckled, and Martha could imagine her rueful expression. "All this energy for something we had all along."

After a few more pleasantries, Martha hung up and then went back to the mind map. She put a small check next to Irma's name. That quilt had been found. So whose quilt did they have? Was it Hazel's, or was it Pearl's? Would they ever know? Maybe she and her sisters would need to be satisfied with the ambiguity of an unsolved mystery.

The next morning Martha dug through the china cabinet until she found a package of floral napkins. The colorful daylilies were bright and seasonal. She checked the table for the fourth time. Elizabeth had set out Mama's best china, with the paper-thin rose teacups and saucers, and the fresh fruit salad with mint that Mary had made was in a lovely antique crystal bowl passed down from Grandma Lois. Martha's scones and muffins were on the table, with Anne's favorite orange and cranberry front and center.

Martha turned to the sink and looked out the window to the tire swing hanging from the enormous old oak tree in the backyard. Daddy had hung the tire when she and Elizabeth were toddlers. It wasn't anything fancy, and through the years he'd replaced the rope a couple of times. Martha wasn't sure how strong the rope was now, but she remembered when she first brought Chuck home from Tabor College to meet Mama and Daddy.

Chuck had been unable to wait a minute longer than he had to, and he talked to Daddy after supper that first night. Then he had taken Martha's hand and led her out to the old oak tree, stood beside the tire swing, and proposed. She smiled, remembering it. Chuck wasn't a man with flowery words. He didn't use any obvious and corny metaphors like swinging through life together or growing their family tree. He just told her he loved her more than he ever thought he could ever love anyone, and then he asked her to marry him. Remembering that moment, Martha felt a tear roll down her cheek. *How I would love to tell him I love him just one more time.* Then she smiled. *Thank You, Lord, for a man who let me know every day that he loved me.*

Mary breezed into the kitchen carrying a vase of daisies and hardy geraniums from the garden. Martha wiped her eyes and turned around, smiling as brightly as she could. Mary set the vase on the table, and Martha was once again impressed with her baby sister's talent with all things color. The flowers brought all the different hues on the table together perfectly.

Martha was just straightening the silverware at each place setting when she heard the front door open. A few minutes later Elizabeth ushered Betty into the kitchen. The Amish woman looked resolute as she walked through the door. Then she stopped, and her mouth formed an *O*. "The table is lovely, Martha. You've gone to so much trouble."

Elizabeth smiled as she stepped in the dining room. "It's no trouble, Betty. This is a day to celebrate." She leaned closer to Betty as if sharing a secret. "I think Martha's been looking for an excuse to break out her inner Martha Stewart."

"I am not sure who that is, but I am glad, because it is beautiful."

A minute later, there was another knock at the front door. Mary hurried past. "I've got it."

In no time, Anne was walking toward them dressed in an elegant dress that had a square neckline and a skirt that looked distinctly like something Grace Kelly would have worn.

"Anne, you are sheer elegance." Elizabeth leaned in to give her a hug.

"This old thing?" She grinned at them and then tilted her head so they could see the tiny pillbox hat. "If I don't play dress-up now, I'll run out of opportunities."

Martha gave her a quick hug as well. "I could learn a lot from you."

"That's the purpose of friendship, dear." Anne seemed to notice Betty for the first time. Her smile stiffened slightly, but then she relaxed her shoulders. "Betty, it's so good to see you."

Martha glanced at Mary, whose eyes were shining. "We're so glad you both could come." She motioned to the table. "Please, sit down."

Mary and Elizabeth helped the older women with their chairs as Martha poured hot water from the kettle into the teapot. She placed the tray holding the teapot, sugar, and cream on the table. "We have miniature cranberry orange scones, blueberry scones, pumpkin muffins, and a short-bread cookie. There's plenty of everything, so please, help yourselves."

Betty's gaze shifted from the food to Martha. "You made all of this since last night? I am impressed."

"Don't be. I would have made the scones and muffins any-way. And Mary made the cookies and the fruit salad. The tea is English breakfast. If you prefer something else, I can make individual cups."

"Well, I'm impressed too." Anne reached for a cranberry muffin. "This all looks wonderful. Thank you, Martha. Thank you, Mary." She turned to Elizabeth. "And don't think you're getting out of this. I know you worked hard also."

Soon the china plates at each place were filled with different bite-sized treats and the matching bowls with fruit salad. When the eating slowed, Anne wiped her mouth with her napkin. "Do you all have any more news about the quilt?"

"Yes and no." Mary stood and a minute later returned with her mind map, which she reattached to the kitchen wall. They'd taken it down for the tea. "These drawings show what we learned as we were researching the quilt." She quickly recounted their trips to the estate liquidator, reading the letters, and Martha's research at the library.

Martha jumped in. "Then there were our conversations with you and with Katie Filbrun Lapp's granddaughter, Charlotte Hawkins. Between you two"—she pointed to Anne and Betty—"and Charlotte, we've accounted for three of the quilts."

Betty looked at Anne, her eyebrows raised. "You found your quilt also?"

Anne smiled at her. "Yes. I feel so foolish. One of my cousins has it."

"And I found mine too. It is with my sister-in-law, Ruth." Betty frowned and spread her hands wide on top of the table. "I am sorry for all the trouble I have caused when the quilt was in the family all along."

"It's all right, Betty." Elizabeth leaned over to pat the woman's hand. "It's easy to lose track of things like that."

"But here I was making it out to be something so important to me when I could not even keep track of where it was."

"Your memory was jogged when you saw the quilt at Secondhand Blessings, that's all." Anne tried to comfort Betty, but Betty swallowed hard, and Martha suspected she wasn't thinking about the quilt anymore.

"Anne." Betty looked to Martha, who clasped her hand and squeezed. "I need to apologize to you."

"Whatever for?"

"I have not been a good friend to you for longer than we were friends, something I very much forgot how to be."

"I left." Anne said the two words like that explained everything.

"But I was so jealous."

Anne stared at Betty. "Jealous? Did you want to leave too?"

Betty swallowed and then set her free hand on her kapp as if ensuring it rested in place. "No. I loved Aaron."

"My Aaron?" Anne's eyes grew round. "I don't understand."

"I told Aaron I wanted us to be together. When he told me he loved you, I blamed you for stealing him from me. I even blamed you for his leaving the church." Betty hung her head. "I knew Aaron was not happy with our lifestyle, but I thought I could make him happy." She looked up at Anne, tears in her eyes. "I knew you did not make him leave the church. I am sorry for harboring such bitterness against you."

"I had no idea." Anne's words were barely a breath.

Martha held hers as she waited to see what Betty would say next. So far, it hadn't been easy, but it hadn't been terrible either.

"Please forgive me for allowing my pride to come between us."

Anne pushed her chair from the table. She stood and walked around the table to Betty, then rested her hand on her shoulder. "It is already forgiven. I'll admit I am surprised, but it explains much of the hurt between us and why it would grow."

Betty stood, and the women embraced. Martha felt tears collect in her own eyes. Then she glanced at her sisters and noticed moisture in their eyes too. After a moment, Mary stood and grabbed a tissue box. As she handed out the tissues, the women started to laugh, and it was as if a pressure point had released for Betty. There was a sincerity in her face and a sliver of joy that was slipping over the hardness. It was beautiful on her.

"Thank you for forgiving me."

"I wish I'd known the cause." Anne went back to her chair. "I had no idea you had feelings for Aaron."

"He did not either. He was caught off guard when I told him how I felt." She sighed and wiped under her eyes. "I should have known then that it was nothing more than a young girl's wishful thoughts."

Everyone sat back down, and Martha drew their attention back to the map on the wall. "I've checked off Irma's, Melinda's, and Katie's names on the chart. So the quilt we have is either Hazel's or Pearl's." She sighed. "I don't know how we'll ever know which one of them made it."

Elizabeth shrugged. "Even if we did know, it wouldn't make any difference. We wouldn't have any way of knowing who to contact about it." She looked around the table. "And now that we know the history of the quilt, I hate to sell it."

"I have an idea." Mary raised her hand as if that would give her the floor. "What if we donated it to one of the local museums as an example of Amish quilt-making from a century ago? We could include the information we have on the circle."

Martha smiled as she considered. "That's a really good idea. I like it better than either selling it or keeping it to ourselves."

Elizabeth stood and pushed her chair in. "I'll take Betty home," she said. "But I like that idea, and it gets my vote. I think it would be a great way to preserve the quilt and the letters and let the most people enjoy it."

Martha looked at Anne and Betty. "What do you ladies think?"

Anne clapped her hands together. "I think it's a wonderful idea. It's an amazing way to let people know about these girls, their friendship, and the quilts."

Betty nodded in agreement, and Mary said, "It sounds like we can consider this mystery solved."

Martha thought for a moment. She guessed Mary was right, but it was a little bit unsatisfying, and she said as much.

"But we did find Betty's and Anne's and Katie's," Mary said. "And a beautiful relationship was mended." She smiled at Anne and Betty.

Martha nodded. "That is worth everything. And I do have to admit I enjoyed learning more about you ladies and the circle letter writers."

As she watched Anne, Elizabeth, and Betty leave a few minutes later, Martha smiled to herself with misty eyes. Surely, the girls from the quilt circle all those decades ago would be amazed at how their venture still brought people together a hundred years later.

CHAPTER THIRTY-FIVE

After supper that night, the sisters gathered in the living room to read Anne's letters. Martha and Elizabeth sat on the couch with the quilt between them, and Mary curled up in the armchair with Tinkerbelle snoozing beside her. Martha picked up the bundle of letters and untied the ribbon. "Should we do the same as we did before? Just divide them and take turns reading them out loud?"

Elizabeth nodded. "That sounds good to me." Mary agreed, and Martha split the letters into three stacks.

She handed a stack to each sister and then picked up the first letter on her stack. "This one is from Pearl." She looked at the date at the top—February 27, 1921—and started reading. *"I am sorry it has taken me so long this time to send our letters along. I have not been very strong this winter, and Maam makes me rest more than I want to. Although usually she is right, and I feel better after doing so. I hope to work on my squares this week and be able to send them to you soon. I am afraid you are all getting ahead of me!"*

The next few letters the sisters read were recitations of what life was like on a daily basis for Amish girls in the early 1920s. While the girls lived in different places, some in the city and some in tiny towns, their days were filled with similar accounts of chores, family, and church. Some of the girls were already looking forward to their rumspringas, and confided in each other their worries about older siblings who were exploring the world beyond their simple life.

Martha came to the last letter in her pile. There were three sheets of paper, all written in the same hand, and not one she recognized. "This is strange," she said. "It's dated November 14, 1922, and it's from"—she looked at the bottom of the page—"Norma Beiler." She began to read.

"*Dear girls, I am so sorry to have to tell you this, but our dear Pearl passed away unexpectedly a month ago. I am sure she told you that two years ago we had scarlet fever in our family. Pearl dearly loved her little bruder, Jacob, and insisted on being the one to care for him through his illness. He could not have had a more gentle, faithful nurse. What we did not realize was that the fever must have weakened her heart, and while she survived the initial bout of fever, the damage to her heart was too great. She grew weaker as the months passed, until finally, she was bedridden, and she passed away one night as we slept.*

"*I am enclosing the squares for your quilts. As I sat by Pearl's bedside these last few months, I stitched them for her. She so wanted to be a part of the "joy" quilt, and we talked many times about each of you girls and the verses you were stitching. She was able to start one of them, but only one, before her eyes grew too weak to see her work.*

"*Oh, girls, I cannot tell you what comfort and peace these verses gave me through each stitch. One of the verses Pearl chose was Psalm 30:5, "Joy cometh in the morning." Through each stitch of the five squares I felt my heart yearning for that morning, for that joy. I know Pearl has gone through the dark night and is now living in that morning joy.*

"*The second verse, Revelation 21:4, was one of Pearl's favorites, "And God shall wipe away all tears." Whenever Jacob fell down or was rebuffed by his older bruders and ran to her, his cheeks wet from crying, she would dry his tears and tell him that someday God would wipe away all his tears, and he would never have to cry again. A few days before she died she saw tears on my cheeks and reminded me of this promise. It pleased her so to see each square as I finished it.*

"'Then I came to the square that Pearl had started to stitch before her eyesight failed her—John 3:29. I had just finished the flowers edging the border, and woke up the next morning to find that our Pearl was gone. She had been talking and laughing with her bruders and schwesders the day before, and we were all heartbroken that she had died without her family around her. It was days before I could take up my needle again to continue my work on her square.

"'When I did, my heart was full of pain, and I asked Gott to help me learn this lesson in Gelassenheit, to help me accept this blow that came before I was ready, that came while I was not there. And He began to speak to my aching heart. Pearl had already stitched the words "This my." As I stitched the word "joy," I heard Him say, "Pearl is my joy, and Pearl is your joy." As I stitched the word "is," I heard Him say, "is, not will be but is. Right now. At this very moment." Then I stitched the word "fulfilled," and I heard in my heart, "I have supplied the missing parts, I have completed the work." And then I realized, Pearl did not need my comfort as she entered heaven. She is complete, she is joyful, she is fulfilled. Gratitude filled my heart with every square as I slowly worked through each word, again and again, and by the fifth one, I could lay my questions and regrets down and trust in Gott's faithfulness to His Word.

"'Girls, it might seem strange to you, a grown woman of our faith sharing her struggles to trust Gott and learn another lesson in Gelassenheit. But I feel as if Pearl would want you to know that your quilt has brought hope and joy to our family when we so badly needed it.

"'I look forward to receiving your squares so I can complete Pearl's joy quilt. It will always be a reminder to me of friends and undying faith in our Lord.'"

Martha looked up from the papers, her eyes wet with tears. Gratitude and Gelassenheit. Chuck was her joy, he was God's joy, and he was fulfilled. Nothing was unfulfilled, nothing was incomplete. Almost a hundred years after Pearl's mother wrote those words, Martha could also lay her questions and regrets down and trust in God's faithfulness to His Word.

She pulled the quilt toward herself and unfolded it to find the square with the verse, "This my joy therefore is fulfilled." She traced the words with her finger, the stitches starting out rough and uneven and ending smooth and uniform. "And now we know," she said to her sisters in a hushed voice.

"This is Pearl's quilt."

CHAPTER THIRTY-SIX

Toward the end of the week Martha took the quilt to the Lancaster Mennonite Historical Society. The curator was thrilled to accept the quilt and letters. Anne had understandably wanted her letters back, so Martha had provided the museum with photocopies. She had made copies of Melinda's letters also, before giving the originals to Betty. As much as the sisters wanted to keep the remaining letters, they knew that they belonged with Pearl's quilt. They made copies for themselves and gave the originals, along with the writing desk, to the museum.

When she returned to the shop, Martha donned her apron and replenished the display case with the baked goods she'd brought earlier that morning. Mary finished waiting on a customer and came over just as she was finishing up. "Before you close that, hand me a cookie, would you?"

Elizabeth joined them and started grumbling something about eating up the profits again, but Martha noticed she didn't refuse the half cookie Mary offered her.

Mary asked around a mouthful of chocolate, "How did it go at the museum?"

"Just fine," Martha said. "I met with the curator, who's also one of the archivists, and she loved the story of the quilt. It took me a while to take her through all our twists and turns, and she said she'll need to contact us when she gets ready to prepare the display."

"Did she say how long it'll take before they'll have it ready for viewing?" Elizabeth brushed the cookie crumbs from her fingers.

"She said it'll be a while, probably a few months. They have to take measures to preserve the quilt when they mount it, and they have to print and mount the signage. Plus, they have to fit it into the rotation of the exhibits they already have scheduled. Oh—and they have to restore the writing desk to its original glory."

Mary wrinkled her nose. "Aw, I was hoping to go see it soon."

Martha came out from behind the display case. "If the next three months are anything like the last three, little sister, you'll be too busy to worry about it."

"Speaking of that," said Elizabeth, "Have you two given any more thought to my idea about hiring someone to help us out here when one or two of us need to run errands or go some-place like the museum?"

"I have," Martha said. "And I must agree with you. Maybe Rachel would know someone we could hire."

Mary frowned at them. "Well, as usual, I'm the last to hear about things around here. I'm assuming one of you was sup-posed to let me in on this."

Martha pointed at Elizabeth and said, "She—" at the same time Elizabeth pointed at Martha and said, "She—"

Mary burst out laughing. "I may not know anything about what goes on around here, but I'll be the last one standing after you two get done with each other." She held up her hand. "And, for what it's worth, I agree with you. We could use another pair of hands around here sometimes."

Elizabeth spotted a customer at the counter ready to check out and said over her shoulder as she walked away, "We can talk about hours and pay tonight at supper."

Mary went back to the display she'd been working on, and Martha tore a couple of paper towels off a roll to clean the window of the baked goods case. As she sprayed the glass and got busy with the toweling, her thoughts went from the quilt and the letters to Norma and Pearl, and then to Chuck. She had made a copy of Norma Beiler's letter for herself before she gave it back to Anne, and she marveled at God's care for her, that He had given her a gift on the very day she needed it most. *Lord, I lay my questions and regrets down and trust in Your faithfulness to Your Word.*

All things were complete. All things were fulfilled. God truly would wipe every tear from her eyes, and joy would come in the morning.

ABOUT THE AUTHORS

Tricia Goyer

T ricia Goyer writes out of her passion for God and her love for family and others. The author of more than seventy books, she writes both fiction and nonfiction related to family and parenting.

This *USA Today* best-selling author has also won two Carol Awards and a Retailer's Best Award. She was also an ECPA Gold-Medallion Nominee and a Christy Award Nominee and won Writer of the Year from the Mt. Hermon Christian Writers Conference.

Tricia's contemporary and historical novels feature strong women overcoming great challenges. She recreates historic wartime eras with precise detail through comprehensive research and is a beloved author of Amish fiction as well, having written the Big Sky series and Seven Brides for Seven Bachelors series.

Tricia is a popular conference speaker. She has spoken at events such as MomCon, Raising Generations, and Teach Them Diligently conferences and been interviewed by numerous national TV and radio programs and magazines. Her new podcast, *Walk It Out*, can be found on iTunes or downloaded on any podcasting app. Whether through writing, blogging, speaking or podcasting, Tricia loves sharing messages of inspiration and hope.

A homeschooling mom of ten, including seven by adoption, Tricia is also a grandmother of four and wife to John. With a busy life, she understands the importance of making every word count.

Cara Putman

Cara Putman is a homeschooling mom of four who is married to the love of her life. An award-winning author, Cara has published over twenty books and is an attorney and lecturer at Purdue University. She blogs at the following sites: TheGroveStory.com, InspiredByLifeAndFiction.com, TheWritersAlleyBlog.com, and CaraPutman.com. She also serves on the executive board of American Christian Fiction Writers (ACFW), which is a great resource for anyone who longs to write fiction.

MORE TO THE STORY
The Biblical Tabernacle Reproduction

In this story, Mary and Bill go on an outing to Lancaster County's Mennonite Information Center in order to see the Biblical Tabernacle reproduction that is on display there. The Biblical Tabernacle is a full-size replica of the original tabernacle, which Moses constructed for the nation of Israel. An on-site lecture tour of the tabernacle explains its history, construction, and spiritual significance.

This reproduction was originally created in the late 1940s as the "Moses Tabernacle in the Wilderness," by a Baptist minister in Florida. Mennonites later purchased the replica and eventually joined it with the Mennonite Information Center. This exhibit has been invaluable for students of Bible and cultural studies for more than sixty years now and thousands of people visit the exhibit each year.

The tabernacle replica is housed in a building with an upwardly contoured ceiling and pleasing acoustics. Tour guides versed in the scriptural context and significance of the tabernacle and its contents lead groups from the bronze altar, just inside the eastern gate of the courtyard, to the Ark of the Covenant in the Holy of Holies. As one looks into the Holy Place, a full-size wax figure of the high priest presides over the altar of incense. His authentic robes have precious stones embedded in gold on his breastplate. The Golden Lampstand, and Table of the Bread of the Presence are made to scale. The temple veil, its design extensively researched, represents the separation of the people from the presence of God, as we learn about in scripture. Many people of diverse religious, ethnic, and cultural backgrounds find this lecture tour the high point of their visit to Lancaster County.

FRESH FROM
RACHEL'S KITCHEN

Rachel Fischer's Chocolate Friendship Bread
(A two-part recipe)

Friendship Bread Starter

Rachel loves to extend a hand of friendship to all she meets...
along with something scrumptious from her oven. She is happy
to share this recipe for the starter base that can be used for a
variety of homemade breads.

1 package (.25-ounce) active dry yeast	3 cups flour, divided in thirds
¼ cup warm water (110 degrees F)	3 cups sugar, divided in thirds
	3 cups milk, divided in thirds

In a small bowl, dissolve yeast in water. Let stand 10 minutes. In
a 2-quart nonmetal container, combine 1 cup flour and 1 cup
sugar. Mix thoroughly or flour will lump when milk is added.
Slowly stir in 1 cup milk and dissolved yeast mixture. Cover
loosely and let stand until bubbly. Leave loosely covered at
room temperature. You can also use a sealed ziplock bag, but
be sure to let the air out of the bag if it gets too puffy. This is
day 1 of the 10-day cycle.

On days 2 through 4: stir starter with a wooden spoon. (Always use nonmetal containers and utensils.) Day 5: stir in 1 cup flour, 1 cup sugar, and 1 cup milk. Days 6 through 9: stir only.

Day 10: stir in 1 cup flour, 1 cup sugar, and 1 cup milk. Remove 1 cup to make your first bread, give 2 cups to friends along with this recipe, and the following chocolate friendship bread recipe from Rachel Fischer's recipe box. Store the remaining 1 cup starter in a container in the refrigerator, or begin the 10-day process over again, beginning with step 2.

Amish Chocolate Friendship Bread

This is Phoebe Fischer's favorite recipe for friendship bread, which her mom taught her to make.

2 cups flour
1 cup sugar
1½ teaspoons baking powder
½ teaspoon baking soda
1 teaspoon salt
1 package (5.9 ounces) instant chocolate pudding mix

1 cup Amish friendship bread starter (see previous page for recipe)
1 cup vegetable oil
½ cup milk
3 eggs
1 teaspoon vanilla or almond extract

Preheat oven to 350 degrees. Lightly grease two 9×5-inch loaf pans.

In a large mixing bowl, stir together flour, sugar, baking powder, baking soda, salt, and chocolate pudding mix. Make a well in the center of this mixture. Add friendship bread starter, oil, milk, eggs, and extract; mix well. Pour batter into prepared loaf pans.

Bake in preheated oven for 60 minutes or until a toothpick inserted into center of loaf comes out clean. Cool on a wire rack before removing from pan.

Read on for a sneak peek of another exciting book
in the Mysteries of Lancaster County series!

Mixed Signals
by Beth Adams

Elizabeth Classen watched as the barns and farmhouses
rolled by through the glass. These roads were as familiar
to her as her own skin, and she loved seeing the countryside go
past. Lights were coming on inside the homes, shining through
windows with a warm glow, and quiet was settling over the
fields and barnyards as Amish farmers led their horses inside for
the night. She loved the familiar rhythm of it. But with each
field and farm that passed, she was that much closer to the
night ending. A part of her dreaded reaching home.

She glanced over at John. His mouth curled up in just a
hint of a smile as he drove. John had invited her to join him at
a Lancaster Symphony concert in a park in Lancaster. It had
been a nice evening and they'd had great conversation and lots
of laughs, and now he was driving her home. They sat in comfortable silence. She loved that he didn't feel the need to fill
the quiet with senseless chatter. There was something wonderful about a friend you could be quiet with. A *friend*, she
reminded herself. Nothing more.

They were about to pass the Hostetler farm, which meant
they were just a few miles from the family farmhouse she now

shared with her two sisters. But as John made a right turn onto the rural road that led over the creek and toward her home, something caught her eye.

She narrowed her eyes. "What is that?"

John slowed the car. "I have no idea."

The long country road stretched out before them, gathering shadows as the summer evening turned into night. Cornfields ran as far as the eye could see on both sides of the road, and the rolling hills of the quiet Pennsylvania countryside gave the whole scene a peaceful, wholesome feel.

"It's some kind of light," Elizabeth said, gazing down the road. What in the world? It looked like the light was coming from the ground, and it was blinking on and off.

"Almost like a strobe light," John confirmed.

"But it's coming from the ditch." As they got closer, Elizabeth could see more clearly that the blinking white light was coming from some kind of device by the side of the road. But what was it, and why was it there? The sky was a deep royal blue, edging toward black, and the soft breeze rustled the dark cornstalks. As night settled in, the blinking white light seemed eerily out of place.

John slowed the car to a stop and then put it in PARK. "Stay here," he said, unbuckling his seat belt. But Elizabeth pushed open her door and stepped out after him. John Marks might be a member of the East Lampeter police force, but Elizabeth wasn't afraid of a little light. She stepped out of the car onto the soft grassy shoulder and followed just a few steps behind him as he moved toward the strobe's source. It had been a wet week, and the ground felt spongy underneath her feet.

"It's a phone," John said, crouching down. Elizabeth came up beside him and saw that he was right. An iPhone lay face-down on the slope of the culvert, blinking a bright white light on and off rapidly from the camera lens. She stepped forward and reached for it, and John put his arm out to steady her as she bent over the sloping dirt side of the ditch.

"Who would leave a phone by the side of the road?" Elizabeth picked up the phone and straightened up. "Especially one that looks as new as this one." She turned it over in her hands. It looked to be a newer model iPhone and had a sparkly pink case. These things were expensive.

John didn't say anything for a moment but looked around, surveying the area.

"Is anyone out there?" he called, looking off into the rows of cornstalks. They were only about waist high but densely planted and could easily hide a crouching person, Elizabeth thought with a shiver. But the only answer was the hum of cicadas.

John turned around in a circle, looking at the ground. His headlights illuminated a small patch of dirt at the side of the road, and John walked over now to look.

"What do you see?" Elizabeth asked.

"Tire marks," John said, nudging the soft earth with his toe. "Someone peeled out of here in a hurry."

"And left their phone behind," Elizabeth added.

"Yes." John nodded. "Though I'm guessing they didn't intend to do that."

"I'm sure you're right." People these days were all but surgically attached to their phones. She couldn't imagine someone would leave it behind on purpose. She touched the smooth round button at the bottom of the phone's face, and the screen lit up, showing a dark field with a white disk in the middle. "And I'm sure whoever owns this phone is missing it. So how do we figure out who to return it to?"

John didn't answer for a moment. He studied the phone, which was still blinking a light on and off in some kind of pattern.

"What is it?" Elizabeth prodded.

There was a strange look on John's face, and he was staring off into the cornfield once again.

"I'm just trying to figure out what happened here," he said, and he reached his hand out, silently asking her to hand him the phone. Elizabeth gave it to him, and he tapped the circle on the screen so the light turned off.

"People don't often just drive away and leave their phones behind," Elizabeth said.

John waited a moment before answering. The rising moon sat low and large in the sky, casting a silvery light over everything. He tapped the screen again, but a lock screen came up, and John was prompted to type in a passcode to access the phone.

"That's true, but I think it's more than that," John said. He was turning in a slow circle again, looking carefully in every direction. He took a few steps, and Elizabeth saw that he was moving toward the bridge that ran over the small creek a hundred feet or so down the road. Elizabeth followed behind him and watched as he used the light on his own cell phone to illuminate the area under the bridge and along the creek bed.

"What is it?" Elizabeth asked again. Something was putting him on high alert.

"I don't see anything here," he said, turning back toward the car.

"What were you looking for?" she asked, coming up alongside him as he turned again, searching in the distance.

"I'm not sure," he said.

Elizabeth felt frustration rise up in her. Was he being purposefully obtuse? What wasn't he saying?

"John." She tried to keep her voice calm and level, even as a bit of fear began to thread through her. "What's going on?"

John stopped next to the spot where they'd found the phone. He let out a long, deep breath.

"I'm not sure," he repeated. "Maybe nothing. But I worry something bad might have happened here."

She had started to feel the same way herself, and the way he was acting wasn't helping. But she tried to keep calm. "Why do you say that?"

"You know that flashing light that attracted us here in the first place?"

She nodded.

"It wasn't just blinking a random pattern. It was Morse code for SOS."

A NOTE FROM THE EDITORS

We hope you enjoy Mysteries of Lancaster County, created by the Books and Inspirational Media Division of Guideposts, a nonprofit organization that touches millions of lives every day through products and services that inspire, encourage, help you grow in your faith, and celebrate God's love in every aspect of your daily life.

Thank you for making a difference with your purchase of this book, which helps fund our many outreach programs to military personnel, prisons, hospitals, nursing homes, and educational institutions. To learn more, visit GuidepostsFoundation.org.

We also maintain many useful and uplifting online resources. Visit Guideposts.org to read true stories of hope and inspiration, access OurPrayer network, sign up for free newsletters, download free e-books, join our Facebook community, and follow our stimulating blogs.

To learn about other Guideposts publications, including the best-selling devotional *Daily Guideposts*, go to ShopGuideposts .org, call (800) 932-2145, or write to Guideposts, PO Box 5815, Harlan, Iowa 51593.

Find more inspiring fiction in these best-loved Guideposts series!

Secrets of Wayfarers Inn

Fall back in history with three retired schoolteachers who find themselves owners of an old warehouse-turned-inn that is filled with hidden passages, buried secrets and stunning surprises that will set them on a course to puzzling mysteries from the Underground Railroad.

Sugarcreek Amish Mysteries

Be intrigued by the suspense and joyful "aha" moments in these delightful stories. Each book in the series brings together two women of vastly different backgrounds and traditions, who realize there's much more to the "simple life" than meets the eye.

Mysteries of Martha's Vineyard

Come to the shores of this quaint and historic island and dig in to a cozy mystery. When a recent widow inherits a lighthouse just off the coast of Massachusetts, she finds exciting adventures, new friends, and renewed hope.

Patchwork Mysteries

Discover that life's little mysteries often have a common thread in a series where every novel contains an intriguing mystery centered around a quilt located in a beautiful New England town.

Mysteries of Silver Peak

Escape to the historic mining town of Silver Peak, Colorado, and discover how one woman's love of antiques helps her solve mysteries buried deep in the town's checkered past.

To learn more about these books, visit Guideposts.org/Shop

Sign up for the Guideposts Fiction Newsletter
and stay up to date on the books you love!

You'll get sneak peeks of new releases, recommendations from other Guideposts readers, and special offers just for you . . .
and it's FREE!

Just go to Guideposts.org/Newsletters today to sign up.

Guideposts®

Visit Guideposts.org/Shop
or call (800) 932-2145